The
Custodian
D. A. O'CONNOR

The Custodian

D. A. O'Connor

PUBLISHED BY
Educate.ie
Walsh Educational Books Ltd
Castleisland, Co. Kerry, Ireland
www.educate.ie

PRINTED AND BOUND BY
Walsh Colour Print, Castleisland

CONTENTS

ACKNOWLEDGEMENTS

This book would never have taken form or appeared before your eyes without the generous help and expertise of the following people:

Sixth class in Durrow National School; staff of Durrow National School, especially the typists, Bríd Brennan, Seán Óg Hynes, Margaret O'Reilly and Teresa Screeney, parents of the writers, Transition Year students, who wore down their fingers typing, especially Áine Green who came in for an extra week; Anna McDermott, who logged all our mistakes; Brian, Mary and Conor Burke, Liam Clavin, Una and Jessica Mullery, Laurence Murphy, Frank O'Brien and Eoin Wyer; Safie Maken Finlay, our brilliant and patient editor; reviewers Aiden Barry, Eva Barry, Eoin Colfer and Claire O'Brien; our patient (really patient!) sixth class teachers, Niall Breslin aka Bressie, Enrica Cullen, AnneMarie Gaughan, Colm Larkin and John Russell; County Photos; Tullamore Credit Union; The Bridge House Hotel; Midlands 103; Betty Kenny, The Wicklow Heather, Laragh; our editor and proofreader at educate.ie, Fiona McPolin; Paula Byrne and Jim McGann at educate.ie; David Kelly aka Senor Tastey, for graphics.

They say it takes a village to rear a child. The same is true for the effort from so many in supporting the authors of *The Custodian*. Thanks to you all and especially to our families.

D. A. O'Connor, aka Niamh Bracken, Frank Crossen, Robert Crossen, Frank Kelly, Robert Kinsella, Elysha Maken Finlay, Molly McNally, Kate Molloy and Jack Wogan, the authors.

PROLOGUE

It was dark and cold. Ronan stood beneath the tree, its leaves providing hardly any shelter from the pelting rain. He fought the pain of the bullet wound in his leg. A gang member, on a mission to eliminate him and take his jewels, lay dead at his feet. Another was wounded, incapable of any further action. They should have realised that he wasn't going down to a bunch of amateurs. He put a hand on the dead man's shoulder and whispered softly.

"Sorry, but I have to continue the work of my ancestors. No hard feelings. Well, you couldn't have, could you, because..." An icy feeling came over Ronan. He pushed it to one side and focused on the task at hand.

The watch on the man's wrist beeped once. Ronan glanced at it. Eight o' clock already!

"Sorry about this," he muttered as he began to switch their possessions.

Watches switched. Shoes switched. Coats switched. Then came the hardest part. Ronan pulled the wedding ring from his finger. It was made of solid gold and engraved with the words, *I will always love you.* He stroked the script and with a heavy heart, slid it onto the thief's finger. The ring was a little too big, but hopefully they wouldn't notice.

"Okay," Ronan muttered, "I can't believe that I'm actually going through with this, but..."

He took a lighter out of his pocket and flicked it on, then lowered it to the man's coat. The flames from the two litres of accelerant he had poured over the body quickly spread. Ronan got to his feet and started walking away, but made the mistake of looking behind him at the blazing corpse. The body was twisting in the flames and the odour of burning clothes was truly horrible. Ronan turned, ran to the other side of the field, and threw up, the sudden realisation of what he had done hitting him like a fist in the gut. He had killed a man.

***

Colette paced up and down the cramped room, her arms folded tensely, constantly glancing at the silent phone. She stared blankly at the children playing on the rug. They liked it here, where it was warm and safe. They didn't seem to be affected by the ordeal they had been through only a few days before. They had no idea what could have happened to their father. But Colette was waiting for the call, the call that had the potential to change her life forever and the lives of her children. When the phone rang, she reached out a shaking hand and answered it.

"Hello?" she said nervously.

"Mrs Colette O'Connor?"

"Speaking."

"Detective Inspector McNally here. Ah, we have found your husband, but..."

"But?"

"I'm sorry."

She slammed down the phone and felt her legs go from under her. As she dropped heavily onto the floor, the two children jumped on her playfully, thinking it was just a game. Oh, how she wished it was.

- 1 -

PIMPLE FACE

Blood is hard to wash off. Matt dabbed at his swollen nose, wincing in pain as he did so. He walked over to his computer, opened PenChat and went through the messages. Spam mostly. He deleted them one by one. When he was finished, he began to compose a message to his best, and only friend, Noname101. That was not his real name of course, just his nickname. This was the only person Matt had kept in touch with since the move.

'I was just wondering,' Matt typed, 'can we call each other by our real names?'

Almost immediately, another message appeared on the screen.

'Nah,' it read, 'it's kinda cool calling each other by code names, like spies'.

'Sure,' Matt replied. He heard his sister, Rachel, calling his name from downstairs.

'I have to go, see ya.'

Matt knew he couldn't tell his sister about being beaten up by the school bullies. He would have to stay quiet.

As he made his way downstairs, Rachel called his name again, this

4

time angrily. Matt presented himself at the doorway with his head down, waiting for the insult he knew was coming.

"Matthew O'Connor, where...?" she turned, "oh, there you are. What happened to you? You look awful... well, worse than usual, I mean".

Matt continued to stare at his feet.

"Is that blood on your shirt?"

Still, Matt didn't lift his head.

"God, you're always getting beaten up." Rachel sounded more frustrated than angry. "Please, don't tell me I'm going to have to look out for my wimp of a brother like before. I had hoped we could turn over a new leaf in this school. Matt, look at me, I'm trying to get through to your thick brain."

Matt looked up sheepishly as his ranting teenage sister rattled on.

"Maybe if you got a bit of muscle, you'd stop being such a walking punch bag. What am I going to do with you?"

Matt didn't know how to answer that, nor for that matter, did he see the need to. There was no point arguing with Rachel. He had learned that it was just better to let her stop in her own time... which she did. She turned her back on him and yelled up the stairs. "Mum, dinner's ready. Are you coming down?"

The two siblings waited until they heard a faint voice. "Can you bring me up some please?"

"Well I can't," Rachel snorted, shoving their mother's bowl into Matt's hands. "I'm not the bloody waitress."

Matt picked up his own bowl as well as his mother's and made his way back upstairs, careful not to spill anything.

Steaming hot soup. De-lic-ious. For all her faults, Rachel was a good cook. Matt was thankful for that, because she seemed to do all the cooking these days. He walked up to his mother's door, putting down both bowls so he could open it.

Matt's mother was lying in her bed.

"Thanks Mattie," she greeted him, although she still seemed half asleep.

Mattie: Her name for him. No one else called him Mattie.

He picked up the bowls and crossed over to the bed, setting his mother's down beside her on the bedside locker. He looked down at her, hungry for any sign of affection, and was eventually rewarded with a very faint smile. This meant a lot to him.

Matt left his mother and went into his own room; his own little world. He flopped down on the bed and reflected on his first few days at Tullamore Comprehensive. Matt had hoped to grow taller now that he was in First Year, but no such luck. He was still smaller than most of the boys in his class and even many of the girls.

Just before school had ended that day, some boys from another stream in First Year - great, hulking, bulked-up boys who looked as if they had gone crazy on steroids - had waited until the final bell rang and everyone was leaving and then cornered Matt in the corridor, shouting taunts at him. Matt had tried to escape, but the boys caught him easily, one of them pushing him over, causing the nosebleed. He had scrambled to his feet and walked away slowly to show he wasn't afraid. What had hurt most was not the nosebleed but the chorus of jeers that rang in his ears as he went.

Why did they pick on me? he wondered. *How did they know I was so defenceless? How do they always know?*

Matt sighed, got up, and went over to his desk. He stared sadly at his soup, which was now almost cold.

"At least you can't laugh at me," he whispered and plunged his spoon in.

***

That night, Matt couldn't sleep. He felt as if something strange was about to happen. He got out of bed and stood for a long while looking out of his window. In the distance, he could see a row of trees that were part of a large area of woodland. On the other side of those woods, he knew, was Elves Quarry, and then Durrow Abbey, his former home.

A fog was rolling across the expanse of houses and parkland between Matt and the woods. It came in sweeping folds, as if it had a life, a momentum of its own. It wrapped itself around trees and buildings, and it wrapped itself around the town. Matt stood for some time, as if mesmerised by the strange phenomenon, before going back to bed. Once there, he rolled over and closed his eyes, but still couldn't get to sleep. *Maybe I'm hungry*, he thought. *Very likely.*

Just then he heard a voice that seemed oddly familiar, but he didn't know where it was coming from.

Maaaaaathew, Maaaaaathew

"R... Rachel," Matt called out in a shaky voice, "stop trying to scare me. I know it's you!"

I am nooooot Raaacheelll, it echoed.

"Whaaaaaa?" Matt screamed. He jumped under the covers, shaking all over. Eventually he poked his head out again.

"Casper?"

Noooooww, nooooww. Maaaaaathew coommmeee and get meee.

"HELP!" Matt squealed. Nobody came. The voice stopped, and Matt drifted into an uneasy sleep.

The next morning, while Matt was getting ready for school, he stopped briefly to check his PenChat inbox.

No messages from my pen-pal today, he thought. *I'll send him a quick one before I go.*

'Hi,' he typed. 'Getting ready for school. Another day of First Year. Chat to you soon. Bye!'

"C'mon Matt," shouted Rachel, "we'll be late".

"Coming," he answered, grabbing his schoolbag and plodding, heavy-footed, down to the kitchen.

***

"Now Matt, you know the drill," said Rachel, as they made their way through the gates of Tullamore Comprehensive. "After school, I want you to show me the idiots who tripped you yesterday. But during school, do not talk to me and do not look at me, unless it's an absolute emergency. Have you got that?"

"I know, I know. Don't look, don't talk," Matt mumbled under his breath.

Once inside the school, Rachel went straight to the lockers where a group of her newly-made friends were huddled together. Ignoring Matt, she began chatting to them. Matt found his way to his own locker, which was on the other side of the corridor.

I've got History, then English, then Maths before lunch, he said to himself, taking out his books and scrutinising the map he had of the school layout.

The bell rang.

Okay, where is the History classroom? He was worried. *Come on Matt, remember... come on. Why do they always have to make these maps upside-down.*

He looked around. The corridor was now empty, apart from Rachel and her friends. They walked past him as they made their way to class.

"Ah... um, Rachel," Matt interrupted, "where's the History classroom?"

Quickly, Rachel pulled him to one side.

"What part of 'do not talk to me' don't you understand? Huh? Go down the corridor and take a left. It's room 31."

Rachel smiled at her friends over her shoulder and mouthed, "I don't know this guy, he's a total freak," before turning around and walking away.

Matt scurried off to find his classroom.

Matt was smaller than average for his twelve years, and he was awkward rather than sporty. His slumped shoulders and sad eyes seemed to hint at a burden that no boy his age should have to carry. The many hours spent in his own company left him less able to make friends the more time went on. His big, creased clothes always seemed to hang off him, giving him a clumsy, disorganised look.

"Room 29, 30, ah... room 31!" he said, just a little too loudly, as he walked in the door.

"Good morning class," said the teacher cheerfully.

Matt sat down and opened his book, but it didn't take long for his mind to be on anything except the History lesson. He was reflecting on the recent encounter with his sister, when his teacher interrupted his thoughts.

"Matthew O'Connor, have you been listening to a word I've been saying?"

Matt looked up at the teacher, Mrs Gaughan, and blinked in confusion.

"Um... yes," he answered.

"All right then. Pray do tell us all what we were just talking about."

"Um... the Celts?"

The class sniggered and turned to stare.

"No, we were talking about the history of Durrow Abbey, a subject you, of all people, should be familiar with, given your family history," Mrs Gaughan barked. "Please pay attention!"

Matt usually loved school and paid attention to his lessons, but today his mind was too preoccupied by the bullies, his bedridden mother and the fact that his sister was driving him crazy. And now, there was this loaded comment from Mrs Gaughan. Why did she have to bring him into it?

As Mrs Gaughan began to discuss the class trip to Durrow Abbey, something suddenly clicked in Matt's mind, something that was not a complete memory, but images and snippets that came as if from nowhere. He remembered an old man and woman, a big house and a doll... no, not a doll; a dummy... a ventriloquist's dummy.

"I... I do remember Durrow Abbey," Matt piped up, suddenly. "My grandparents used to live there, and I did too, when I was young. I did a lot of exploring, and I found a dummy, Mr Freckles. I played with it every day, but I lost it. Once, when I was in bed, I heard a strange voice calling my name. It told me to come and find it..."

For a moment, Matt was lost in a world of his own again before he realised the mistake he had just made. Mention of his early childhood home always brought him trouble and immediate scorn from his mother and sister. Now he had a new, awe-struck audience. *Not good. Outside voice, inside voice*, he thought.

"There have been legends of a haunting at Durrow Abbey," Mrs Gaughan said, "and that terrible business that involved your family, but you, Matthew, must learn to separate fiction from fact".

"That... that must be my dummy. It has to be!" said Matt, more to himself than to the class, every one of whom was now looking in his direction. Many of them were smirking at each other.

"Now Matthew," one cheeky boy called out, in a squeaky voice, "you must learn to separate fiction from fact".

The class laughed.

Although she had only been teaching Matt O'Connor for a few

days, Mrs Gaughan had noticed that he carried a worry on those slumped shoulders and possibly some sad secret behind those downcast eyes that made him stand out from the others. She realised that the last thing he needed was his teacher providing his possible tormentors with further ammunition.

"Come on class, settle down. My apologies for involving you, Matthew," she said sincerely. "As I was saying, the class trip to Durrow Abbey will be on October 4th. Don't forget to get those permission slips signed."

Matt was at the gates, waiting to catch the school bus home, when they appeared, strolling down the school path, laughing and jostling each other.

"Look at little Mattie, the boy who lost his dolly, waiting for his Mummy to collect him," jeered the lead loudmouth, whom Matt had christened Pimple Face. "What? Is your daddy not around to take you home?"

Matt knew better than to reply. He put his hands into his pockets and stared up into space.

"Sorry for involving you, Matthew," Pimple Face taunted, in a poor imitation of Mrs Gaughan's voice.

"Is there something wrong with your voice, Miss?" Matt answered, drawing a burst of laughter from Pimple Face's sidekicks.

"Did he just cheek me?" Pimple Face asked them, cutting their chuckles short.

"He sure did," replied a vacant-faced, lanky boy.

"He's gonna pay for that!" Pimple Face shouted.

Matt turned to run, but just as he did so, a fist crunched into his face.

- 2 -

DURROW ABBEY

Everything was blurry, but Matt could hear footsteps growing increasingly fast as they faded into the distance. He felt a hand slap his face, and his vision sharpened. A tall girl was standing over him.

"Oh my God, Matt. Are you okay?" It was Rachel.

"Yeah, I'm okay," Matt mumbled groggily.

"Get up!"

"Jeez Rach, I'm trying."

On his third attempt Matt stumbled to his feet. The world swayed alarmingly, and he heard a ringing sound in his left ear. Rachel grabbed his arm.

"Matt, what happened to you?"

"The zit head and his gang. Someone hit me."

"They punched you and knocked you unconscious?" For a moment Rachel looked genuinely frightened, but then she became angry.

"Matthew O'Connor, you are such a wimp! Why do you have to provoke them?" she shouted.

Matt did not bother answering. It would just make her angrier. It seemed to him that Rachel was always angry now, in the months since their mother had stopped getting out of bed.

Rachel sighed, "Matt, this has gone too far. When we get home, I'll have to give you some serious pointers."

Uh oh, Matt thought, *what's she gonna do now?*

Ten minutes later, they were in their own kitchen, their schoolbags dumped in the corner. Rachel was sitting at the counter.

"Right Matt, show me your walk."

"My walk?" *Has she finally gone crazy?* he thought.

"Yes, your walk. Now walk to the other end of the kitchen."

Feeling stupid, Matt trudged over to the window and back.

"No, no, no, no, no!" Rachel barked, exasperated. "No slouching, stop dragging your feet! Walk the walk! Back straight, head held high!"

"Seriously? I don't want to look like a model, I'm not a girl!"

"There are such things as *male* models you know."

"Ha. They wear more makeup than you do!"

"Just walk!"

"Fine!" Matt was so busy concentrating, he tripped over the rug. Rachel giggled, "You might want to look where you're going."

"Thanks for the tip," Matt grumbled.

After a while, Rachel and Matt retired to the couch with a bowl of crisps.

"Listen up," said Rachel, "I'm only going to tell you this once. You need to change your image. I'm serious when I say you should walk tall and proud. Remember you are a direct descendant of the last High King of Ireland, Rory O'Connor."

"Not that again. He's not here to defend me. Besides, I'm covered in bruises!"

"Fine, but I'm not finished. You have to look this guy in the eye. A confident person will not be bullied."

"Okay?" Matt seemed a little unsure.

"And also, don't be a loner. Hang out with your little friend, you know that one you sat next to a few times... David. If you are with someone, it will be harder to pick on you. And if you are busy, they can't get you. Besides, he seems like your type." Rachel laughed and gave Matt a friendly push.

"Hey, I resent that insinuation. Take it back!"

"Just kidding bro. And finally, while I am giving you the benefit of my advice, don't forget your secret weapon."

"What's that?"

"Your big sister, stupid. That zit face and his cronies wouldn't stand a chance against me."

"Sure," Matt said uncertainly, trying to clear his mind of the embarrassing image of his sister bashing his tormentors around the corridors of Tullamore Comprehensive. "Oh wait, I think I hear my PC. Gotta go."

Matt stood up, glad of his sister's advice but looking for a way out. He paused before going up the stairs.

"Rachel?"

"Yeah?"

"Thanks."

"Get out of here before I give you a hug, you idiotic brother of mine."

That was all the incentive he needed to sprint up the stairs.

***

Later on that evening, Matt peered into the living room. Rachel was sitting on the couch, arms crossed. She was watching an American comedy, something called *iCarly*.

"Any sign of that hug? Or even dinner?" Matt asked.

She frowned at the intrusion. Apparently her don't-bother-me regime was happily restored.

Oh dear, he thought, *this means I'll be making my own dinner tonight.*

Matt couldn't cook. Even toast ended up burnt when he tried to make it. Sometimes he found it hard to believe that he was related to Rachel, who could have been on *MasterChef*. He decided on a microwaved sandwich, but ended up with something that resembled an explosion on a plate. As he took his first bite, he remembered the permission slip for Durrow Abbey.

Matt went back into the living room. Rachel had turned off the television and was chatting on her phone to someone. He walked over and stood in front of her.

"Rachel?" he asked timidly.

She glanced up at him.

"Sorry Sandy. After swimming okay. Gotta go. There's some person here who wants something." She put the phone down. "What is it?"

Whoa, she's being nice for a change!

"Can you sign this permission slip, so I can go on a school trip to Durrow Abbey?"

"No way! We don't mention that place, remember? You know you promised Mum that we would never go anywhere near Durrow Abbey."

"But Rachel... "

"No buts! Get out of my sight!"

***

A few hours later, Matt was in his bedroom watching a video on YouTube when he heard the familiar voice again, echoing in his mind.

The video was a funny one that had over 100,000,000 hits, and Matt was laughing so much that he almost didn't hear the voice the first time it spoke. Then it came again, louder and clearer.

Matthew, go to Durrow Abbey.

Whoa! Matt pressed a clammy hand to his head and closed his eyes. *Am I hearing things? Who calls me Matthew?*

Deciding that he needed some fresh air, Matt walked to his window and looked out through the branches of the weeping birch tree that brushed the side of his house. The moon was full and peered out from behind the occasional cloud. He knew it was only two or three miles, but he worried about the consequences of disobeying the only strict condition his mother had imposed on him since they moved back to Tullamore; under no circumstances was he to go anywhere near the place where he had lived until he was five.

Matt reflected on why his mother was so dead set against the past and always so reluctant to answer any questions about it. Sometimes he felt as if he had lived his short life in two phases, the early part that he had largely forgotten and the later, struggling part, living with his increasingly withdrawn mother and his feisty sister. He loved them both as well as he knew how, and he knew that, in their own way, they must care for him, but he wondered why it had to be such a test all the time.

Across those fields and through the dark shadow of the woods in the distance, lay Durrow Abbey. In it, Matt thought, there might be some of the answers he needed, answers that might explain why he wasn't living a better life, a life where he knew who he was. Something his History teacher had said on the first day of school came into his head. "Without a past there can be no future."

On the tree-lined roads of the estate, life was boring and quiet. A blue van crawled past the house. It came to rest at the end of Forest View, but no one got out. Matt watched it for a while, speculating on what clandestine operation the occupants might be conducting. He soon lost interest.

Returning to his desk, Matt decided to log in and check if Noname101 was online. He began to compose a message.

'Hi Noname! I just had THE WORST DAY EVER!!! I'm serious!

First daydreams in History class, then bullies and now my sister is blanking me! I wish my dad was here.'

He pressed send and waited. The reply came within a few minutes.

'Hey hey hey! Sorry to hear about your day. Can you tell me the name of your school so I can come and beat the crap out of those bullies?'

'Oh ha ha. Very funny,' Matt typed, 'but, if you really want to know, it's Tullamore Comprehensive. And they're just a bunch of First Years who think they're Second Years. They'll probably get fed up with me after a while. That's usually how it works out.'

'I could send my dad over... Sorry Matt, I didn't mean that. I know your dad doesn't live with you. Is there anyone you can talk to? A teacher, or your mum?'

'No. I can handle it. Don't want to talk about it anymore... so TTMF. Have to go, bye!'

'Before you go, did you find out anything else about your dad?'

'No, but there have to be some answers lying around my old home, Durrow Abbey. My class is going there soon on a field trip, but I might just go over there on a mission of my own.'

'Is anyone living there now?' Noname typed.

'No. We were the last. I hardly remember anything about it. If I visited, maybe it would bring back some memories.'

'You should go.'

'I will.'

'When?'

'Tonight.' Matt thought for a while as he waited for his friend to come back. Then he typed, 'Listen 101, I know you have to be careful on the Internet, but would it sound a bit weird if I asked you for a photo of yourself?'

Matt waited. The two or three minutes that went by seemed more like ten. He was just wondering if he should withdraw the request, or in some way apologise, when a message came through.

'Yeah 102. It does sound really weird, but... here goes...'

A picture of a boy popped up on Matt's screen. The boy, who seemed to be about eleven or twelve, had dark curly hair, sallow skin and a pleasant smile. In the background it was sunny. In the suburban garden, a family gathering was taking place. The boy was brandishing a water gun. He seemed really happy.

'Sorry,' typed Noname, 'it's a bit of an old one of me, a whole year ago. Do you have one?'

Matt searched his files and uploaded one of himself that was also a couple of years out of date.

'Don't laugh, 101. I don't have a recent one either. We haven't been taking many photos around here lately.'

'Ha ha... cool. Now I feel I know you a whole lot better. Good luck on your mission tonight.'

'Thanks.'

Matt logged out and played a few half-hearted games of *Candy Crush*. As he listened to the game's little 'ding dong' sounds, he made a decision.

I'm going to do it!

There wasn't anybody downstairs, Rachel having gone out for

the evening. Matt packed his satchel with some essential supplies, also known as crisps, left quietly by the back kitchen door and was already cycling out of the driveway and onto the footpath when he remembered that he was still wearing his pyjamas. He doubled back and changed into more appropriate attire.

Take two, he thought, as he set off again on the bike.

Ten minutes later, Matt was not sure if this had been such a good idea. He was crouched in a muddy ditch, peering at Durrow Abbey through a gap in the thorny branches. A mist was stealing across the moonlit grounds, giving the place an eerie look. It was cold and dark, and Matt was just about to get up and go home when he heard the familiar voice once again, its long-drawn-out words echoing in his brain.

Commmeeee and fiinnnndddd meeeeee. You are sooooooo clooooossse.

Matt took a fortifying breath and squeezed through the hedge. He trudged across the gravelled path until he arrived at the entrance of the big house. He tried the door handle, but it was locked. Noticing some moss-covered steps to the left of the door, Matt went down them and began to skirt around the edge of the building, along the cut stone wall with its imposing castellations, until he came to an opening in a side wall. He thought this must be some kind of large air vent. One of the vertical iron bars that protected it was conveniently missing, allowing him to squeeze through. When Matt made it through the opening, he found himself in an underground room. Ahead of him was a set of stone steps that led up to a heavy oak door. He climbed them, and a quick try of the ornate iron handle gave him access to a hallway, which, in turn, opened onto a long corridor. Moonlight entered the corridor through a large window at one end. A beam of silvery light fell on a painting on the wall opposite Matt. As he looked at it, the door crashed shut behind him. Without looking back, he ran.

Halfway along the corridor, Matt stopped, panting from the exertion, and leaned against an oak-panelled wall. It was then that he noticed it, a dark bookcase that he remembered from when he was a child. From somewhere deep within him, another memory returned. He pushed on the bottom shelf, heard a familiar click and swivelled the heavy piece of furniture a full 180 degrees. It opened onto a large compartment. As it did so, Matt heard the voice again. This time, it seemed to be louder and more insistent inside his head.

At lassst, you have founnnd me.

Whatever or whoever was making the noise (and Matt had a sneaking suspicion what it was), he was determined to find it.

"What is that?" he called out as he flicked on his torch. "Is someone there?"

The torch's faint beam illuminated the compartment.

From the corner of his eye, Matt could see the huge shadow of a human-like figure, which seemed to raise its arms slightly, as if in greeting. He shone his torch on the figure that stood at the back of the compartment and was paralysed with fear. The figure had a sinister smile on its red painted lips, and a black top hat was pulled down low over one eye, giving it a rakish quality. It was wearing pinstriped trousers and a red-lined black waistcoat, which was missing a couple of buttons. It was covered in a thick layer of dust, and parts of its chipped wooden face had broken off, making it a pale shade of cream. Slapped on its face was an 'I'm-gone-seven-years-and-you-never-even-came-looking-for-me,' expression. It was a doll... no not a doll, a ventriloquist's dummy. It was Matt's dummy.

All of a sudden, Matt's mind was flooded with images from his past. He saw himself running around Durrow Abbey with the dummy under his arm. He saw his sister frowning at the dummy, screaming at him to stop frightening her, and he saw himself yearning for his lost dummy, crying uncontrollably as the policemen whisked him off in their car. Matt realised that what he had thought was movement had just been the dance of shadows in the beam of his torch. He almost laughed with relief, but then he heard the voice in his head again.

My friend, my kin, you are not alone. There is another here of skin and bone.

Frowning, Matt decided to bring his long lost friend home. He took the dummy out of the compartment, and folding its legs and arms as best he could, stuffed the lower half of the dusty, wooden body into his backpack, leaving its head and shoulders hanging out.

Matt was just turning to leave when he heard a voice, and this time it was not coming from inside his head. It seemed to be coming from a room just to left. Matt pressed his ear against the wall.

"Where is that little twerp?" someone was muttering. "The minute he finds what I'm looking for, he's dead!"

Matt gasped. He couldn't be sure, but he thought the voice was talking about him.

How many boys could be wandering around Durrow Abbey at this time of night? He wondered to himself.

It had been a man's voice. Matt did not think it was anyone he knew, but one thing was for sure, he didn't want to meet him.

I guess I'll have to find another way out, he thought. Something squirmed in his satchel, and he dropped it in fright. *Okay, did my dummy just move?* he thought. The voice in his head spoke again.

End of the corridor and take a right, to avoid the man who comes in the night.

Matt had no time to consider his options. He picked up the satchel and ran to the end of the corridor.

Hmmm, dead end, he said to himself. *That's weird.*

The wall at this end of the passage was bare apart from a thick velvet curtain. Matt pulled the drapes apart to reveal a painting of a familiar couple on their wedding day.

"I wonder who they... wait... they must be my grandparents," he whispered.

Well, I suppose that makes sense, he thought. *They did live here after all.*

There were no doors at this end of the corridor, just bare walls. Matt examined the blank patch of wall to his right and realised that it was not completely bare. Low down on the wall, there was a shape. It was a hand print.

Maybe I have to put my hand on it, he thought.

The man's voice was growing louder, and strange, uneven footsteps could be heard, coming closer. Praying that it would work, Matt placed his hand against the print on the wall. It fitted perfectly. He pushed gently, the stonework giving way to his touch.

There was a loud noise, and a section of the wall swung open. Matt ran through, pushed the section back into place and found himself in the grounds of Durrow Abbey. He ran to the ditch and climbed through, making his way to the place where his bike rested against a tree trunk.

As he cycled home, Matt thought to himself, *So I have a walking, talking dummy with a built in Sat-Nav system. Cool!*

∗∗∗

When he got home, Matt nearly fell through the front door in his eagerness to get inside. Once in, he slumped against the door and took several deep breaths. He unzipped his backpack and pulled out the dummy. It was exactly how he remembered it, more jaded and dusty, but there was no doubt, it was his dummy. Memories from his childhood raced through his mind, shocking and momentarily paralysing him.

He remembered hearing his Mum and Dad arguing heatedly while he had been slumped against the stair railing, not wanting to listen but unable to tear himself away. He remembered clutching the dummy's hard, smooth body for comfort as tears trickled down his cheeks.

A weak voice called from upstairs, startling Matt back to reality.

"Who's there?"

"Mum, it's me, and I've got something interesting," Matt answered.

"Oh, hi Mattie. Is it food?"

"No, just something I found."

25

"You can tell me about it later, Mattie. I was hoping Rachel was home, so I could finally have some dinner."

"No, just me."

"Tell Rachel I want her when she comes in... please."

"Yes, I will."

Suddenly deflated, Matt trudged upstairs. The first thing he saw when he opened his door was his computer screen flashing. He had a message. He slipped into his chair and opened his inbox as fast as possible.

'Hey man,' Noname had typed, 'did you go to Durrow Abbey??? Find anything cool?'

Matt was about to reply when everything went dark. The only light came from the pale rays of moonlight shining in the window. The monitor of his PC extinguished itself with a beep.

"A power cut?" Matt muttered to himself. "Crud!"

"Mattie," his mother's voice drifted across the landing, "my bedside lamp's gone out".

"Coming Mum. I'll get some candles from the utility room."

Grabbing the torch from his backpack, Matt went downstairs to examine the junction box. A quick glance told him that something had shorted the system. He flicked up the switches one by one, and power was restored. He knocked gently before putting his head round the door of his mother's bedroom.

"No need for the candles after all. Can I get you anything?"

A feeble voice came from beneath the pillows and the mess of bedclothes.

"Just Rachel when she gets back. And... thanks Mattie."
Matt retreated, closing the door softly as he went.

- 3 -

THE DELIVERY MAN

S aturday night found Matt bored and hungry. He had finished the homework he had given up on the previous night, and Rachel had gone to the cinema with her boyfriend to see *The Lone something-or-other*. He had looked for food, but there wasn't even the tiniest of crumbs, and he couldn't face his third bowl of cereal in one day. Sometimes, even when his mum had been in bed for a long stretch and Rachel hadn't shopped, a bag of groceries would magically appear on the kitchen counter. This hadn't happened for a few days now, though. Matt had asked his mother about this, but like everything else he asked her, she simply shrugged it off.

There was no money in the house, apart from Matt's precious savings, but hunger wasn't excuse enough for him to dip into these. To top it all, the dummy was not talking, if talking was what it was doing, so Matt was unable to have another telepathic conversation. *This could be a very dull night*, he thought.

He checked his computer to see if Noname had replied to his last message. The inbox stayed resolutely empty, however.

"Aaw," said Matt, his shoulders slumping. Hearing a motorbike stop outside his house, he looked out of the window. It was Rachel and her boyfriend... what was his name again? More importantly, who cared? The guy put his arm around her and... ewww! Matt averted his eyes. Talk about gross.

A few seconds later, Rachel stalked inside.

Matt counted down in his head, *three... two... one...*

"Matt!" Rachel bellowed. "Get down here."

When Matt came into the kitchen, she thrust a package at him.

"For dinner," she muttered and left the room, heading upstairs.

Matt slumped into a chair at the table and opened up the little bundle. His eyes lit up... leftover chips and bread and butter. He gulped it down so fast that he could hardly taste it. Oh well.

There was a knock at the door.

Matt answered it. A man in dark clothes and mismatched runners stood on the doorstep. He held the handles of some large shopping bags in his hands.

"Hello," said the visitor.

"Hi. Who are you?"

"I'm from the pharmacy at the hospital," the man explained. "I'm delivering medication for Colette O'Connor. I'm assuming you're her son".

"Yes. I'm Matt."

Matt turned and called upstairs.

"Mum! Someone to see you. Name of... what's your name?" he asked the man.

"Ricky Moseley," the man answered smoothly, stepping past Matt and into the hallway.

"Ricky Moseley," Matt called. "He's delivering your medicine. Oh... and Rachel, can you come down please?"

Matt returned to the kitchen and hastily swept the greaseproof package into the bin. The stranger followed him awkwardly; he seemed to have a slight limp. He placed the deliveries on the kitchen countertop.

"I'm afraid I can't offer you anything. There's nothing to eat or drink," said Matt.

Ricky Moseley swept his eyes over the kitchen appraisingly.

"So I see. That's why I brought you these."

Ricky Moseley began unpacking the large shopping bags. Matt could see that they were overflowing with groceries. He decided not to ask any more questions.

Rachel arrived in the room.

"Thanks," said Matt in relief. He used her presence to disguise a gradual retreat towards the stairs.

"Hello sir," Rachel said to the visitor, taking the large white box that he'd pulled from one of the bags. "Thanks for these, and the food. I'll unpack them, thanks. Mum said there'd be a delivery. How many of these tablets does she have to take?"

"One with each meal," the man answered, with a thin, unconvincing smile. "And these few things are for you kids. I met your mother a few times when she called at the pharmacy where I work. She might have mentioned me?" He continued to unpack the groceries.

Matt found that he did not trust the visitor. There was something less than genuine about his smile. Ricky Moseley was a skinny, scraggy man of about 45 years. He had long, thinning hair and an unshaven appearance, not the sort of person who would work for a clinic or a hospital, Matt surmised.

When his question drew no response from either Matt or Rachel, Moseley continued even more unsteadily. "We spoke a few times and she... ah... asked me to call. It's just that we haven't seen her in a few weeks and I thought..."

"Thank you very much," Rachel said, politely taking control of the situation. She held the kitchen door open for him, and Moseley took the hint and left.

Matt was glad when Rachel closed the front door behind the stranger. He relaxed as he watched the blue van pull away from the kerb.

"Did Mum mention that she had met that guy?" he asked Rachel.

"No. But I'm not arguing with all this nosh, are you? Besides, there's enough blue and white inhalers in here to treat your asthma for a whole year." She shot him a 'why-argue' look and a shrug of her shoulders that signalled the subject was closed.

"I didn't like the look of him very much," Matt said.

"Is that why you asked him into the kitchen? '*I'm afraid I can't offer you anything,*' she mimicked. "When are you going to learn how to deal with people?"

Later on, in the sanctity of his bedroom, Matt saw that the dummy had moved from its usual place on top of the bulging laundry basket and was now staring at him from the chair at his desk.

To answer your question, I found the odour of fermenting stockings and under garments most disagreeable.

"I didn't ask," Matt replied, closing the door behind him.

Forgive my candour, but in my know-how-ish sort of way, I get the distinct impression that I have encountered that obnoxious being on some vaguely remembered occasion in the past. What, if I may be so bold as to enquire, was the nature of his business with your household?

"Creepy delivery guy," Matt answered, "with medicine for my mother."

He has a worrisome aura about him. I do not trust him, and if I were you, young Matthew, it's a close and a curious eye I'd be casting in that one's direction.

"How do you know? You didn't even see him."

One does not have to behold with the human eye to determine the irksome primitiveness of the fellow. Not to mention the tenuity of frame and shifty curiosity he bore about his person. Would you not agree?

"If I knew what you were on about I might agree, or not. He kind of gave me the willies."

Again we are at variance, Master Matthew, and will remain so unless you can muster some semblance of proficiency in the vernacular, let alone command of the language itself. What are these so called 'willies' that he has bestowed upon you?

"You know, the willies, the creeps. Okay, so neither of us likes the guy, I get it. At least I now know that you must be talking to me, if that is the right word, 'cause I couldn't make that stuff up, not in a million years."

Indeed you could not.

"Can you explain why you wouldn't communicate with me all day and now you seem to have exploded with talk?"

I thought you would never ask, dear Matthew. He who thought it not agreeable for man to be alone was not mistaken. When you sorely abandoned me on that fateful night seven years ago amid the flames and pandemonium, and condemned me to share a damp room with none but clambering frogs and scurrying creatures for company, you almost wiped all semblance of routine; of day and night, of bedtime and play time, from my memory. I am not so quick as to recover and turn on my charms like a chorus girl enduring her burthen of song at the Palladium. No, my young friend. I am not like your Peecee friend where you can strike the power button and have me produce my nuggets of wisdom and insights. And when you condemned me to the darkness of your wardrobe for all of yesterday, only to resurrect me to be seated this afternoon on the glory of your dung hill of a laundry basket, then I chose not to speak - and indeed that is the correct word - with you.

"Ah, sorry I asked."

And.

"And what?"

Matt sat staring at the wooden, garish face in search of a clue, but none came. Then it dawned on him. "Ah that's it. You're jealous."

Wrong.

"Okay, I get it. You're afraid of the dark."

Wrong.

"Okay. I'm sorry I left you in the dark in the wardrobe. I'm not ashamed of you. As for the other stuff you mentioned, I haven't the foggiest notion what you're talking about.

Thank you.

"Don't mention it."

***

In the kitchen, Rachel was just finishing putting away the groceries when her mother appeared. Rachel was surprised to see her, standing beside the countertop, holding onto it for support. It was a few days since Rachel had seen her mother out of bed, and she noticed that she was looking much older than before. Colette had turned 39 the previous July. Her long, blonde hair hung in unwashed, limp clumps around her tired, worn face. Her eyes looked dull and almost colourless in their shadowed pockets. Her dressing gown was wrapped warmly around her.

"Mum!" shouted Rachel, giving her mother a big hug.

"Careful, careful!" said Colette. "I am much too weak for all this hugging."

"Sorry. How are you?"

"Tired and drained, but these meds are a lifesaver, thanks to our delivery man. I wanted to see him."

"Mum, ever since Dad disappeared, you've been shutting yourself away from us and the world. You said the move back to Tullamore would be good for us. I'm not sure if it has been. There's a whole world outside your bedroom, you know. Matt and I are really trying to make ends meet here. And do you know something, Mum?" Rachel was whispering now. "Matt keeps talking to himself. I've heard him chatting away in his room when there's no-one else there. I think he has imaginary friends or something."

"Rachel, he's twelve now, nearly thirteen. He doesn't have imaginary friends."

"And I think he's being bullied at school. Actually, I know he's being bullied. I want him to sort it out for himself, otherwise it'll be just the same as before. But I'll tackle the little freaks if I have to."

"No Rachel," Colette said wearily, "better if I can talk to someone, call them. Strange, Mattie never mentioned it".

"He hasn't had a chance. Besides, he just hopes it will all go away by itself. The principal wants to arrange a meeting with you. You should go."

"Hey kid, that's a lot of information in one go. I'll go. Of course I will, if I'm up to it."

"And Mum," began Rachel, "I think that Moseley guy fancies you."

"Well aren't you the observant young lady. What makes you say that, Miss Nosy Parker?"

"He didn't need to call personally with your stuff. And the groceries! Is it him who's been leaving food parcels?"

"What food parcels? There aren't any food parcels."

"What do think I've just stuffed our fridge with? There have been others, on days when it couldn't possibly have been you, when Matt and I were at school."

"He shouldn't do that. I'll talk to him about it." Colette's tone had changed, as if the annoyance it bore could somehow disguise her recent lack of interest in her children and life in general.

Rachel let it slide. She lifted the mood again. "Yeah, Mum, he does fancy you. I wouldn't be surprised if he asked you out. By the way, did you notice how much he was limping?"

"Now leave the poor man's soccer accident out of it and make your mother a coffee."

- 4 -

AGATHA

Matt heard the school bell blare throughout the building; the bell that basically means, 'Get to class before you get left behind in the bustle, idiot!' He dashed over to the locker where he kept his books, but today he wished he had them in his backpack because opening the locker was a huge, huge mistake! He entered his code, pausing to make sure he had entered all the right numbers, and then yanked his locker open. But today was not the usual open-your-locker-grab-your-books-go-to-class day. When the door swung open, he had only a fraction of a second to notice the string attached to it before a pressurised air explosive was triggered, and Matt was covered in flour.

Stay calm, Matt thought. *Wash this off and go to class, then no one will ever know.*

When he turned around, however, it was to find himself surrounded by a sea of people. Many of them were laughing and taking pictures on their phones. Consoled by the fact that digital photos could not ruin his social life considering the fact that he didn't have a social life, Matt pretended that nothing had happened.

At the sink in the toilets, Matt splashed himself with water, ridding himself of the flour that covered his hair. With his hair wet and his head low, he walked into his classroom and took the only seat remaining. He groaned inwardly when he saw that it was right beside Pimple Face and that he would have to inhale his foul breath for an entire class.

Matt's day had already gone downhill, and he still had classes with some of the meaner of his teachers to look forward to. Yes, this was going to be quite a day. The only good thing was that his quick clean up seemed to have taken the sting out of Pimple Face's little prank. The guy seemed almost human. Almost.

Don't get carried away now, he reprimanded himself.

There was no sign of David, a small, stocky, shy boy whom Matt had sat beside in some of his classes, so he spent much of the rest of that long, hard day on his own. When he finally arrived home, Rachel was quick to notice the scowl on his face.

"Fun day at school, then?" she asked.

"Yes Rachel, the bullies turned positive and gave me a cake. Or the ingredients for one! Does it look like I had a good day?"

"I made you some dinner. Take it up with you if you like. But wash up the plate when you come down. I'm going out with Derek."

Matt was thankful for the note of sympathy in her voice.

"Thanks Rach... you're my favourite sister," he joked.

Matt carried his plate upstairs and munched on his food thoughtfully while he waited for his computer to switch on. Thoughts of Durrow Abbey had been on his mind all day. As the desktop came into view and a flashing icon told him that there was a new message from Noname, he resolved to defy all warnings and go there once again. *Rachel is out and Mum certainly doesn't care,* he thought to himself.

Noname's message read, 'Hey, you doing anything interesting? I'm so bored.'

'Hi 101,' he typed, 'I'm going to DA again tonight.'

'Aren't you afraid of the dark? That place would be too spooky for me.'

'Have you been there before? Do you know it?'

Nothing came back for a few minutes. Matt finished the food.

'No,' typed Noname, eventually. 'Did you live there for a long time?'

'No, only when I was very little. I lived there with my family up until the fire that destroyed the stables. But I don't remember that. Besides Mum won't talk about it, so we're not allowed to either. I just looked it up on Google maps, and I'm interested in the little gate lodge at the back. I might just go there, see if anyone lives there and if they know anything.'

'About what? Who do you think lives there?'

'Not sure, but it sort of rings a bell with me, if that makes any sense. No, I know it doesn't.'

'Why does your mum not want you talking about it?'

'Don't know. Rachel goes along with that too.'

'Why did you move back, from Naas to Tullamore?'

'Don't know. I think Mum thought we should face things. That's what she said anyways.'

'Face things. Like your dad going missing. That must be tough?'

'Yeah...' Not sure on how to respond, Matt paused and went to fetch his backpack from his wardrobe. As soon as he opened the door, Mr Freckles toppled out.

"Hi there," Matt said, propping the dummy up on his bed. "Sorry for locking you up again. No choice, old chap. The sister and her house rules, you understand what I mean. I'll just place you here to guard my stuff. I'm talking to my friend."

As Matt spoke, the lights went out again, and the computer screen went blank.

"What the heck?" Matt thumbed the 'on' button on the computer. Nothing happened; it seemed to be getting tired of having to re-boot every time he turned it on. A thought came into Matt's head. He looked over at the dummy, who was staring at him from the bed, his face a picture of innocence.

Freckles! yelled Matt mentally, so loud that his own brain started to hurt.

Yes, the dummy answered.

"It's you who keeps cutting the power, isn't it? Seriously, stop it. It's really, really, annoying."

No need to shout, my dear young friend. It's giving me a dreadful headache. Now let us depart for Durrow Abbey as you have decided and please, do hurry, if you don't mind. People can be frightfully slow.

Matt fetched his backpack and made his way down to the kitchen. He filled a bottle of water and found a rope in one of the cupboards, both of which he packed into the bag. Thinking it would be best to leave a note for Rachel, although he didn't think she was likely to bother reading it, he tore the lid off a cereal box and wrote on it, 'Rachel, I'm gone out, don't worry. I'll be back soon. Matt.'

Ten minutes later, Matt was wheeling his bike through the rusty, old metal gate that led into the grounds of Durrow Abbey. Once he was inside, he knelt down to check the wheel. It was punctured, badly, and his knee sank into cold, squelchy mud, forcing him to get back onto his feet. He brought his bike to the shelter of the trees and tried to prop it up against a tree trunk, but it fell over. Matt gave an annoyed sigh and tried to find a position in which the bike would not topple. This exercise took up the best part of two minutes, and when Matt looked up, he found the area flooded with fog. The trees now seemed like cold, dead hands, reaching out to touch his face with black, leafy fingers. He stumbled backwards, suddenly desperate to get away, only to fall down into a puddle of sloppy, muddy water. It splashed up and covered him from head to toe.

Suddenly feeling very afraid, Matt crawled away backwards. He stretched a hand behind him, but his searching fingers met only air. He twisted his head around and saw a dark opening. Then, he was falling, with his own scream ringing in his ears.

There was a terrible thud, which Matt knew must be his body making contact with something very hard... then nothing, except for an overpowering bolt of pain in his head, more violent than anything he could ever have imagined or experienced before. The pain seemed to be outside of him, as if it belonged to someone else.

Matt became aware of a strange, dream-like sensation. He could see people running through the very passage where he lay. His mother, younger and more energetic than she had been lately, was dragging a little boy and an older girl. They were crying as they ran, and his mother was urging them to be quiet. A wall of smoke was coming down the passage, thwarting them. Yet they raced on and emerged through the smoke, searching for someone. He saw a man framed in a gap in the woods. Someone was following him. The man looked back, clutching a case to his chest, and when he saw the woman and children, he raised a gun and shot it into the air. There were shouts. People followed the man, and Matt could hear more shots being fired. He felt the intense heat, and someone was grabbing them, pulling them away.

The next thing Matt knew, he was lying on his stomach on a cold, stone floor. It was so dark that he could barely see his own hand in front of his face. He tried to sit up but felt instantly woozy and had to lie back down. He groaned. His whole body ached, but especially a spot on his head. He pressed his fingers to it and pulled them away, wet and sticky. His eyes having adjusted to the dark, he could see the red on his fingertips. He gave another groan and, finding an old tissue in his pocket, pressed it to his head.

Where am I? He thought to himself.

Matt managed to pull himself up onto his elbows and scan his surroundings. He was in a passage of sorts, and directly behind him, there was a set of stone steps leading up to an opening. Through it, he could see the setting sun. The passageway itself seemed to stretch on forever and ever. Faced with the options of proceeding down the stone channel or climbing back up the stairs, Matt chose the stairs and started to climb. He felt around and eventually found his torch. Luckily it still worked.

Was I knocked out? For how long? He looked at his watch... almost two hours had passed since he had left home. *Must keep on going. I have to get some answers.*

He walked around to the back of Durrow Abbey, the terror of his dream still with him. *I must get answers,* he thought, *but where? What happened next? Who dragged me away? What was in that case my father held so precious? Why was my father carrying that and not me?*

He was on top of a small, steep hill. He dug his heels into the ground trying to prevent himself from a face-plant, but no such luck, he fell onto the wet grass. Lifting his head out of a small puddle, Matt wiped the water off his face. At least he was now fully alert. He sat up and looked around. The clouds were covering the moon and the leaves of the beech trees swayed in the soft breeze. It was all quite creepy. Matt stood up. He stared at a small oak tree. It seemed somehow familiar. Flashbacks from earlier in his childhood raced through his mind. He saw himself and his family filling a small pot with clay, sitting on the lush green grass with the sun beaming down on them. Matt placed a small acorn into the pot and then his father pushed it softly down through the clay and covered it over. Another memory came of a duller day at a later time. The acorn from the pot had grown into a tree. He could see his father had used a small pocketknife to engrave the words RONAN, COLETTE, RACHEL, MATT on its trunk.

A drop of rain fell on his forehead, and Matt snapped back to reality.

"Crud," he said. "It's starting to rain. I'd better go to the gate lodge."

He ran through a small bundle of briars and one of them caught on his trouser leg. He pulled it off and it made a little hole in the fabric, but he ignored it and kept running. It was starting to hail now. *I need to find some shelter.* Matt ran into the church where the high cross was kept. As he walked up the aisle past several of the pews, something caught his eye. On the side of one of the pews was a name in fancy cursive writing. It read: "O'Connor Family".

"Wow" said Matt surprised, "we must have been very important". He sat down on one of the pews until the hail stopped. Then he went outside and had a look around. He saw a crypt with the words 'O'Connor Family' engraved in the wall. Through the bars, he could see a headstone on which was written 'Charles O'Connor R.I.P'.

"Hey, that's my great, great, grandfather," said Matt, scrutinising the walled enclosure. "Cool."

A laneway led away from the back of the Abbey, and Matt began to walk along it. He was surrounded by whiteness, almost as if it had been snowing, but it was only hail, and it was melting away already. Trees overhung both sides of the lane, and their leaves dripped drops of extremely cold water onto his head. Matt tried to dodge them, but every time he avoided one drop, another fell onto him. When he finally reached the gate lodge, it was almost midnight, and the moon was beginning to emerge again. As Matt approached the neat little stone cut building, a mangy dog began to bark viciously at him, its hackles standing up on its neck. He could clearly make out the glint of the animal's teeth in the moonlight. He froze.

An old, hunched-over lady eventually emerged from the house waving a stick.

"Who are you?" she shouted. "What on Earth are you doing on my porch at this hour of the night? Answer up now or I will use this blackthorn stick on you."

"I... I'm Matt O'Connor" Matt stammered, over the increased barking of the approaching dog.

"What are you saying? Matt O'Connor? Ronan O'Connor's son?"

"Yes, that's me."

The old lady's anger faded. The moonlight glinted on her spectacles as she stared through the darkness at him.

"Why didn't you say so in the first place? Come on in, like a good young man. You'll get your death out there on a night like that."

Matt stepped into the house. It didn't look anything like the outside, which was cluttered and had slates hanging from the roof. Inside, it was tidy and clean, except for the cobwebs that hung in almost every corner. Although the wallpaper was peeling in places, the atmosphere was homely, and the dying embers in the open fire were warm and welcoming.

The old lady silently stoked up the embers, adding small pieces of kindling that immediately took light. Then she filled the kettle, switched it on, and took a seat at the kitchen table.

"Sit down Matt," she said, "How are you? My name is Agatha, but you always knew me as Aggie."

Confused, Matt sat down.

"Hello Aggie."

"Now Matt," she peered at his head, "you don't look too well. That's a nasty looking gash you have there. Are you all right?"

"I'm fine... I think."

"I certainly hope so. I will wrap this little bandage around it for now to keep it clean. I'll have a cup of tea into you now in a few minutes, and you'll feel much better."

"Thank you," Matt said, wincing in pain as the old lady wrapped a rough, white bandage tightly around his head.

"This will have to do for the present time, but you might need the doctor."

"I'm fine, really I am. You said you knew me before?"

"I know a lot about your family. I know about your dad, your dear, beautiful mother, your sister, and of course Mr Tickles. I minded you and Rachel when you were little, so you could nearly call me another member of the family."

"Oh, do you mean Mr Freckles?"

"If that is what you call him now, then yes. Back before you had him, he was Mr Tickles. But it is good to change the name every once in a while. Stops him from getting notions, I suppose."

A click from the kettle signalled that it had boiled. The old lady went through the process of making tea as if it were a sacred ceremony; scalding the brown teapot before spooning in the loose tea from a tin box, which looked familiar to Matt. It had a picture on its side of a woman in a silk shawl. Matt remembered seeing this picture before. Agatha took out two china cups and produced a plate of chocolate biscuits.

Matt sipped the strong, sweet tea and politely took a biscuit. Agatha watched it go down, as if waiting for her chance to give him another one.

"Ah go on, have another one."

He did as he was told.

"So," she said as she sat down again, "many have presumed that your father died on that terrible night but that, Matt is not true. The truth is that he is missing but alive." She peered at Matt over the rims of her thick-framed spectacles, giving her young guest time to digest this news, while she sipped her tea.

"Sorry?" he asked, through a mouthful of crumbs.

"Do you know why he had to flee? Why he had to leave?"

"No. No-one's ever explained it to me."

"Well, to put it simply, your father left to draw the thieves away from his family. In the process, he drew a lot of suspicion on himself, especially with that awful business of the burnt man. It would never have come about if it wasn't for those blackguards who tried to steal your family heirloom."

"I don't understand. What is an heirloom?"

"For many centuries, your family, the O'Connors, have been the custodians, the keepers of a special treasure, which they have guarded and protected, sometimes with their very lives. There have always been those who try steal what doesn't belong to them, and that is what happened on that night. Sadly your father was let down by many in power, and now he has to prove his innocence before he can return to you and your family."

The meaning of what the old lady was saying slowly began to sink in.

"So my dad's not dead after all?"

"Matt, he was injured and he took a long time to recover. By the time he could even think of coming out of his hiding place, he was under as much suspicion as those who had tried to rob him. When one of the robbers was captured, he conveniently implicated your father so as to get a lighter sentence, and your father has been on the run ever since. Many even presumed him dead."

"But he's not. Right?"

Matt thought of the explanation his mother had given him. It had been a lie. Even Rachel must have gone along with it. They had let him think that his father was dead. He hung his head and began to cry. "Let him go," they had both told him. When they had moved back and set up their new home in Forest View, his mother had warned him not to go anywhere near Durrow Abbey. How could he ever look at either of them ever again?

Agatha was standing now, beckoning him to follow her.

"Come with me," she whispered softly.

They stepped outside. Agatha took a torch from her pocket and shone it on a crest that was on the wall beside her front door. In the middle of it was a crown, and on either side were two lines that met at the end and formed an arrow, pointing downwards.

"That is the O'Connor family crest. It symbolises the power of the last High Kings of Ireland, those who have been entrusted with the crown of power. It passed on to your father and to his fathers before him. In time, when this temporary business is sorted out, it will be passed on to you and yours."

The old woman's croaky voice sent a chill down Matt's spine. He didn't know what to say or where to turn to.

"Good boy. Come on in now, and you can have another biscuit."

Agatha brought Matt back into the house and sat him down. If she had left him out there, he would eventually have been standing in a puddle of his own tears. She gave him more biscuits in an attempt to calm him down.

"So he's still alive? You're sure of it?" said Matt between sobs.

"Yes he is. You might be surprised to learn that he has been keeping a watchful eye on you and has been much closer than you think, many times. He has operated, at times from a secret hideout deep in the vaults of your old home and not even I know how to get into it. And you're not to get any fancy ideas either now, ya hear? The last time he was there he wrote you a letter. He asked me to give it to you as soon as I could."

Agatha reached out and lifted a large wooden clock from the mantle-piece. She turned it over and opened the back with a small key that was attached to a chain around her neck. Inside it was a carefully folded piece of paper. The old woman flattened it out and handed it to Matt. It read:

Dear Matt,

If you are reading this then you have met Agatha. She is a very kind woman as you will have seen and knows a lot about our family history. When you were younger, she took care of you, but you might not remember her. By the time you read this, I will have been missing for some time, maybe even years, but please don't think badly of me, although I will understand if you are angry. You will have read the accounts in the newspapers, but none of them are true. All these years, I've been in hiding until such time as I can prove my innocence. If I had surfaced before now, I could have been put in jail for colluding with the robbers; an accessory to a theft I would never have committed! I am writing this because I have something very important to tell you, son, something my father told me when I was a boy like you: we, the O'Connor family, are the custodians of the Irish Crown Jewels. It is our duty and our responsibility to take care of them. We have guarded them for hundreds of years from invaders and pilferers. They were once on display in Dublin Castle, but knowing that thieves were planning to seize them, your great grandfather, who was the custodian at the time, took them away and hid them in Durrow Abbey.

Don't tell your mother about this letter. She will not want you involved, but you are an O'Connor, and protecting the jewels is our sacred duty as a family. Don't tell Rachel anything either. I will find a way to contact her myself. There is no need to worry; I am safe and well, and with your help, I can return to a normal life and the world can know what really happened to our family on that terrible night. Be brave for now, my son, and await my instructions for you. Agatha will let me know you have received this letter. She will know what to do.

Yours truly,

Your loving father, Ronan O'Connor.

Matt held the piece of paper, staring at it, long after he had finished reading it. Tears began to roll down his cheeks.

"Ah now, Matt, don't start that crying again," said Agatha, getting up and handing him a tissue.

"I know," said Matt between sobs. "I'm happy for him because he is alive, but I'm sad because he can't be part of my life while he's still missing. And I'm sad that Mum and Rachel didn't tell me the truth."

"I know, I know," said Agatha, wrapping her arms around him. "Here, save your breath now to cool your porridge. Let's have another cup of tea and then you can set off home."

She made the tea and sat down at the table again. The two of them drank in silence. When they were finished, Matt stood up, wobbled, and sat down again.

"Oh dearie me, you are in no condition to go anywhere, you poor boy."

"No, no, I must get home. I must tell my family!"

"Now steady yourself. That is something you must not do. I will contact your father and let him know that you have his letter. You will have to await his instructions like he said. To do anything else other than wait now would prove a further torment for him. It might well put you, Rachel and your mother in further danger. Come back to me when you're better, and I will know what to do. And remember, you can call on me any time of the day or the night. But it has to be our secret, just for now, you understand? Remember now, any time, day or night. Only, be careful."

- 5 -

CONFRONTATION

Matt made his way unsteadily to the door with Agatha's concerned voice echoing behind him. He walked along the leafy laneway, past the stables, past his former home. When he picked up his bike and began to wheel it out along the avenue, he remembered the puncture.

"Oh, no," he groaned.

He was still sore and bruised, but now two things were taking precedence: the wound on his head and the fact that it would take ages to get home. Thankful that the fog had lifted, Matt left his bike in the shelter of some bushes and stumbled out of the gates.

"Ow!" he gasped. Trying to ignore the pain, which felt as if someone was drilling a big hole in his head, he struggled down the side of the driveway and out onto the main road. All the while, he clutched his dad's letter tightly in his hand. It was the first communication from his father in seven years. Matt was happy with his new-found knowledge, but confused and angry with his mother and Rachel. His sister must have known about this, he thought, and yet she didn't tell him. They had let him think that his father was dead! Matt wondered how he could ever forgive them? He didn't even want to be with them. The bleeding was getting worse, and he felt dizzy. He knew he had to get home... soon.

Much later, a weak and utterly exhausted Matt pulled himself through the door of his house and tried to shout, "Rachel," but all that came out of his mouth was a hoarse squeak.

Rachel had apparently been waiting for him, because she emerged rapidly from the living room.

"Matt! It's nearly two in the morning. Where... what happened to your head?"

"I feel dizzy." That was all Matt could say before giving in to the pain and slipping away into the dark oblivion of unconsciousness.

His sister's concerned voice cut through the blackness. It was followed by a different voice, one that sounded slightly familiar. It was the delivery guy from the pharmacy, Ricky Moseley.

"He's coming round," Moseley announced.

"Mum," Matt moaned. Then he remembered what he had learned and stopped himself from talking.

"I'm here Mattie," said his Mum, "I'm here."

But Matt was already sinking back into emptiness, into something resembling sleep.

He was woken by the sound of Colette speaking. Through his eyelids, he could see that he was lying in a hospital bed. Colette was nearby, gazing at him sadly.

"He looks so still. He will be okay, won't he?" she asked Ricky.

"He may have a slight concussion." Moseley announced, with what

sounded like authority. He gave her a charming smile, "They are not sure."

Moseley was standing a little too close to Colette for Matt's liking. With a moan, he closed his eyes and fell asleep again.

So absorbed was Colette in her son that she completely missed the expression that briefly appeared on Moseley's face. Rachel, who was sitting opposite, noticed that his charming smile had vanished briefly and that his lip curled into what might have been a mocking expression. She gave Moseley a searching look. He seemed normal, she thought, though a little scruffy and thin, but the poorly healed scar over his left eye and the shiftiness that seemed to accompany him gave her the feeling that he was not to be trusted. Moreover, the way her mother looked at him made Rachel feel uncomfortable.

Sometime later, Matt woke up feeling slightly better. He reached up and touched his head, which was heavily wrapped in gauze. His gaze was then drawn to the people sitting beside him.

"Mum! Rachel!"

They both hugged him. In spite of what he had learned from Agatha, he felt warm and safe in their embrace. He only had them to himself for a brief moment, however, before *he* shuffled in, Ricky Moseley, carrying a bunch of flowers and a big chocolate bar. Moseley handed the chocolate to Matt and gave Colette the flowers and a kiss on the cheek.

Matt raised his eyebrows and looked from Moseley to his mother, but his efforts to make sense of the cosy scene were interrupted by the self-assured voice of a doctor who had also entered and was glancing at the chart at the end of the bed. Matt noticed that Ricky slipped swiftly out of the room as the doctor introduced himself and proceeded to give his diagnosis to Colette.

"Your son has had a trauma and some bleeding. My colleagues in the Emergency Department kept him awake for most of the night and morning, and all his vital signs are, quite frankly, perfectly normal. He has slept a lot today, but we have no concerns for him. He is basically good to go."

The doctor looked at Matt.

"Don't you go exploring any more old castles on your own, young man. It looks like you had a whole lot of people worried about you. They told me you were out on your own in the middle of the night on some sort of adventure. Is that right?"

"Yes. It wasn't that late really. It's just that I fell down a hole and bumped my head."

The doctor turned to Colette. "Keep him off school tomorrow, but there's no reason why he shouldn't be back there, right as rain, on Wednesday."

"Thanks doctor," answered Colette.

At six o' clock that evening, Matt was plonked in the back of his mother's old Mondeo, Rachel occupying her natural place in the passenger seat. He was spared any interrogation on the short journey to Forest View due to an incident involving his mother's car and an innocent old lady who was nearly mown down as she tried to negotiate the pedestrian crossing with her wheelie bag. He decided that his mother had to be one of the worst drivers on the planet. This time, Matt was grateful for her awful judgement, although he sensed that, once they got home, he was the one who would pay for the poke of the woman's walking stick against the front bonnet of the car. His mother's silent tension was like the silence of a judge just before passing the death sentence.

Once they were home and all three of them were seated at the kitchen table, Colette stared at Matt as if she were waiting for a full and frank explanation of the previous night's activities. Matt thought about everything that had happened, letting it flash before him until he came to the point where he remembered the note. He gave a little start at the thought but immediately disguised it as a dart of pain. This didn't evoke any sympathy from his mother.

"Matt, I only asked that you do one thing for me when we returned to Tullamore. You and Rachel both promised. You know how hard it was for us in Naas. Here, we had a chance. Me, to get my old job back, so that we could finally make ends meet. I trusted you two to look after yourselves. Now, I know I am not exactly fulfilling my end of the bargain, but I am getting there. With proper medication, I know I'll be working soon, full time. Rachel has been absolutely brilliant. All I asked of you, Mattie, is that you do your study and stay out of trouble. But you haven't done that, and you went there. You went there in the middle of the night without telling anyone where you were going. You could have been killed... What am I saying? You almost *were* killed."

"I left a note," Matt countered feebly. Immediately, he knew this was a bad idea, a really bad idea.

"That's not the point," Colette shouted. "You promised never to go back there, and you broke that promise. Didn't you?"

Matt hung his head. There was so much he wanted to say. But all of it was wrong. Not a single word or memory from the night before could be shared with his mother, and he wasn't sure about Rachel. *They mustn't have found the note from his father*, he thought. *If they didn't, then where is it? What if someone else finds it?* Matt wasn't in a position to do anything about that now, so he did the only thing he could, what he always did when faced with a force greater than himself, he did nothing. "Sorry," he managed to say after a while.

"Sorry? Sorry? Is that all you have to say?" Colette demanded.

Matt stared at a tiny toy aeroplane under the table. He wished that he was small enough to hop inside it and fly, fly to anywhere but where he was now.

Colette sat back in her chair, closed her eyes and groaned, as if the exertion of the day had taken a massively disproportionate toll on her. Rachel, who had responded to their mother's speech with a passive expression, got up and put on the kettle. When it had boiled, she poured the water into three cups and silently piled in milk and sugar. Matt was grateful for her neutrality.

***

"Hi," Matt said, as he walked into his mother's room several hours later, carrying hot tea and some toast with marmalade. "Are you okay, you look a bit..." he paused, anticipating a fight, but he knew he had to have this conversation, "under the weather."

"I'm fine. You know that I haven't been... great. Seeing you in the hospital like that really took it out of me."

Maybe this isn't such a great idea, Matt thought to himself. He began to walk away, but the voice of Mr Freckles urged him on.

Matt, this is a good time to tell her. If not now, when? Moseley is going to come and mesmerise her, and then she won't believe you.

Stay out of this. Give me a chance. It's hard enough without you in my brain, Matt countered.

"Sorry Matt," his mother said sleepily. "Did you come here for a reason? I just had a tablet. They make me a bit drowsy."

It was his mother's eyes that gave her away, told him she was in another dimension, one that didn't include him. The eyes somehow seemed less full than they could be. Softer. Without life. Matt remembered fishing with his father in Elves Quarry as a small child and impaling pike and perch on a sally rod. The point of the stick would be inserted through the gills and out through the mouths. The accumulated catch would slide down along the length of the twig until they would snag on a branch. In the heat of the day the sad, skewered fish would look out at the cruel world that had wrenched them from their existence. It was their eyes he remembered most, large questioning eyes that slowly lost their lustre, grew soft in the hot sun and surrendered to their cruel crucifixion. He hated the comparison, hated the image, now that he had transposed the fish eyes onto those of his mother. Quickly he banished it, focused on the questions he knew he must ask.

"I know, but... " Matt took a deep breath, and wondered how to phrase what he wanted to say. "I need to talk to you about Dad."

"Look, Matt, I feel very tired. Can we do this another time, maybe when I'm better?"

Matt knew what his mother was doing and he understood why, but even though she was depressed about everything, he thought that what he had discovered was too important to let slide. Matt had no intention of telling her about the letter before the time was right, but he wanted to know about the other part of the story, the human part; the Mum and Dad part.

"No, Mum, I have to know what he did to make you want to forget about him."

"It's not that I want to forget, it's just that I don't like to talk about it. Anyway, how could I forget what happened and what he did?"

Matt walked over to Colette's bed and sat down.

"But whatever he did, it must have been for a good reason. And... I met an old woman named Agatha, who..." it had escaped before he could help it. But at least now he had her full attention.

"Where and when did you meet her?"

"I met her at her house when..."

"Don't go back there again, Matt. All that dreaded place has done for us is to bring misfortune."

"But I found..."

"Look Mattie," she interrupted, "you are owed explanations, but please wait until I am ready. Please sweetheart. Until the time is right, please respect my wishes and don't have anything to do with that place. Not anymore, alright?"

"But Mum, all my memories of Dad come from there."

"We may have had a good time there, until he abandoned us to protect his stupid old jewels. I told him that if anybody ever tried to steal them, he should protect us. We had an escape plan, but then there was that awful raid, and they smoked us out. Family was supposed to come first. That was our agreement, but it didn't work out that way." She was becoming increasingly angry.

Matt didn't say anything for a while. He sat on the edge of the bed, staring out into the night sky.

"Matt, at the start of this, I understood why you missed your father, but it has gone too far. Just move on and forget him. I chose to move on with my life, and I demand you do the same. And Matt? Do not even think of going off and finding your dad. If there were any chance that he was still alive, I wouldn't get his insurance money. That's the one thing he's done for us."

"What do you mean?"

"It's been almost seven years, and the insurance company is about to pay out soon on his life insurance, provided you don't go and do something stupid."

"What?" gasped Matt, staring at her in disbelief.

"You heard me, Matt. Your father was insured for the value of a mortgage we took out on that pile of mould and damp where we lived. I never got the pay out because some idiot reported seeing your father escape into the woods with his precious box. His blood was found at the scene, but there wasn't enough conclusive evidence to say that he was dead at the time. So no pay out. In truth, Matt, all I care about now is getting that insurance money. It belongs to us. It's what he left us, to rebuild our lives." She turned her face away from Matt's searching eyes.

Matt couldn't believe his ears. *Did she actually just say that*? He left her lying on her bed, and went to his room.

- 6 -

MATT MAKES A STAND

M att was lying in bed awake. He had to go to school the next morning, and he was thinking about Pimple Face. He was sick of being called names and pushed around by him. It wasn't fair. He had only been in the new school for a couple of weeks, and he couldn't stay under the radar. Rachel had made friends straight away. She was tall and confident. Everything about her - her striding, upright walk, the way she swished her long hair when she turned, the way she questioned everyone, even those in authority (especially those in authority) - gave her a 'don't-mess-with-me' look. Matt had watched her with her new friends. She was a fitter-inner. She knew what to say after 'hello.' She laughed, even if laughter wasn't immediately called for, and she seemed to make people want to be around her.

Matt, on the other hand, never seemed to know much about the topics of conversation that seemed to be flavour of the month. Sometimes he would study up on soccer or rugby just to have something to contribute, but information gleaned from websites was no substitute for having played with the lads on the Naas Rugby team and definitely no substitute for having gone with your dad to see Man-U play at Old Trafford. No, somehow his information always seemed fabricated, borrowed from some wanna-be club that he never could be part of.

Thankfully, he had gotten to know Noname really well. He seemed to be the only person who was genuinely interested in Matt and his family. Noname accepted Matt, challenged him and made him question his past. Sometimes, he seemed singularly curious. His awkward questions had got Matt into trouble with Rachel and his Mum, especially those that delved into the previous life; the one he lived when he was small.

Pimple Face, on the other hand, was bad news. Matt dreaded meeting him in the morning.

Stand up to him. Mr Freckles interrupted his thoughts.

Matt looked over at the desk, where the dummy was perched, its wooden chin resting on its chest.

Say to him, you have no right to talk to me this way. You don't have the right to touch me. Say it louder. Shout it. Say, you don't have the right. You don't have the right.

Matt sat up and switched on his lamp.

"You don't have the right to talk to me that way. You don't have the right to touch me," shouted Matt loudly, repeating the words Mr Freckles had spoken to him in his head.

"Shut up Matt!" groaned Rachel from the other room.

"Oh, sorry Rachel." Matt switched off his light and closed his eyes.

When Matt finally got to sleep, he had a dream, a good dream. He dreamed that he was in school, and Pimple Face was about to punch him when he shouted, "You have no right to talk to me that way. You have no right to touch me." Pimple Face got so embarrassed that he left the school and the town. In the dream, everyone cheered Matt and put him on their shoulders.

"Matt, Matt, Matt, Matt!" they chanted.

He was woken by Rachel's angry voice.

"Matt!" she called. "Wake up!"

Matt got up.

"Okay," he said to himself, "I've got to do it."

While he was eating his breakfast, Matt heard the voice again.

Remember, you don't have the right.

As he walked into the school hallway, the words, "you don't have the right" were still echoing through Matt's head. They were beginning to freak him out, so he tried to think of something else. Unfortunately, the only other thought that came into his mind was an image of Pimple Face punching him so hard that his head fell off.

"Ow!" Matt winced at the very thought of it.

"Talking to yourself, runt?"

Matt didn't have to turn around. He knew who it was. The self-assuredness he had felt earlier suddenly faded.

"What? You're giving me the silent treatment? C'mon runt, I can't live with that," Pimple Face crooned sarcastically.

Jerk, Matt thought.

What he said out loud was, "You don't have the right."

"What?" Pimple Face asked stupidly.

Matt swung around to find that Pimple Face was just inches away from him.

"You don't have the right," Matt repeated. He started shouting it, screaming it at Pimple Face, who was suddenly looking quite spooked.

"YOU DON'T HAVE THE RIGHT! You do not, I repeat, do not have the right to humiliate me. Step off! YOU DO NOT HAVE THE RIGHT!"

By now, the hall was full of staring students. Pimple Face tried to salvage the situation and bring it back to something he understood.

"Whoa," he said, "someone pack this guy off to the loony bin!"

Nobody laughed. A teacher came hurrying up.

"Is this young man bothering you?" he said to Matt.

Matt nodded.

"He was the one yelling like a nutter," spat out Pimple Face angrily.

The principal marched up to them, steely faced.

"Dinglefitz! My office, now! And you, Matthew O'Connor, you too."

In spite of the seriousness of the situation, Matt couldn't resist a grin as they were marched along the corridor. Pimple Face's real name was Dinglefitz? Ha!

Once they were in his office, the principal talked to them both in a calm, serious tone, addressing Dinglefitz first.

"I've had more trouble from you in the last couple of weeks than we've had from all the other students in a year," he said. "As such, starting next week, you will be suspended for three days. I have already spoken to your mother, and she is on her way to collect you."

"But please Mr Watson, my dad will kill me and..."

"Another word and I'll make it a week. Now sit outside my office until your poor mother gets here. She can entertain you for the next three days, thank you very much. Report to me immediately after assembly next Monday."

Matt was secretly delighted. No Pimple Face for three whole days? Awesome!

Once Pimple Face had left the office, the principal spoke to Matt.

"Just a few words, Matthew. Sometimes I refer people to our school counsellor, Caroline. She's quite good at solving pupils' problems. It's actually her job. I'll make an appointment for you, let's say, for two o' clock this afternoon. I'll give your mother a call and let her know what's happening. Are you happy to see her?"

"If you think it's the best thing to do," Matt said resignedly.

At break, Matt was standing alone in the lunch hall, looking for somewhere to sit, when he noticed David, the shy boy who sometimes sat at his desk, standing beside him.

"Matt, th... that was very brave of you," David said. "I always get bullied, but I'm not brave enough to stand up to them like you. You're like a hero."

"Really?" Matt asked, looking very surprised. "I don't know why I acted like that. I didn't mean to. A wave of anger just came over me."

"Whatever it was, it worked. Ah... mind if I sit with you?" asked David.

"Of course not. I've never had anyone to sit beside me at lunch before. Well, not since coming here."

The two boys found a table and sat down together.

"Hey Matt, wanna trade your chocolate sandwich for my boring stuff?"

"Sure," Matt smiled. *My first real friend*, he thought, *and as a cool perk he trades my soggy sandwich for his delicious crackers and cheese with butter. Real butter!*

"Mmmm, this is lovely!" said David, taking a bite of Matt's sandwich. "I haven't seen one of these since I was in Primary."

"I made it myself, a speciality you know," Matt said in his best Heston Blumenthal voice. They laughed, all thoughts of the principal's office momentarily forgotten.

Out of the corner of his eye, Matt caught sight of Rachel as she walked past with another girl. When he made eye contact, he was rewarded with a little raise of her eyebrows which seemed to indicate approval for a change. This gave Matt an even better feeling than the one he was getting from the crisp, dry crackers and the creamy cheese and butter.

"You fancy a coke?" David asked, rising.

"Ah, I don't have..." Matt began.

"No worries, mate," David chirped, in a poor imitation of an Australian accent, before skipping up to the dispensing machine. "I'm not good with bullying types but I know all about machines. Watch this."

Matt was amazed to see David boldly walk up to the vending

machine, wait until he thought no-one was watching, then with an expertly aimed kick at its side, produce a can of coke. The thump caught the attention of the security man who immediately challenged the machine-battering boy.

"Hey, Crossen, what do you think you're up to?"

"Sorry Mr Bracken, but I paid for two cokes and only one came out."

"How many times do I have to tell you kids? One at a time." Although complaining, the security guard took out a set of keys, opened the door of the vending machine and handed David a second can of coke.

The sight of the enthusiastic fetcher returning with the drinks brought another wide-eyed glance of approval from Rachel, who was sitting across the cafeteria and had witnessed the entire performance. Matt raised his drink to her as a salute, but she dismissed this communication, turning again to her friends.

As they munched on their lunches and drank the cokes, David took Matt by surprise when he asked, "Would you like to come over to mine sometime?"

"What?" Matt looked puzzled.

"My house. Do you want to come to my house? Play some games or whatever?"

"Oh, right. Sure. You can come to my house sometime too. I've got loads."

"Okay well... how about Friday? I'll go to yours and then you can come to mine."

"Sure!" Matt smiled. "Friday sounds good."

At five minutes to two that afternoon Matt walked down the corridor to the school counsellor's office. He took a deep breath and knocked. Almost instantly, it was opened by a pretty woman in her late twenties. She held out a hand for him to shake.

"Hello!" she smiled, "I'm Caroline. How can I help you?"

"Uh, hi. I'm Matt. The principal told me to come down..."

"Ah, Matt, come in, come in. Make yourself at home."

The office was surprisingly comfortable. There were two armchairs facing each other over a low coffee table littered with arts-and-crafts pieces, and there was a big shelf lined with board games. Caroline seated herself elegantly on one of the chairs. Matt flopped down onto the other.

"So, Matt," she said, clipboard in hand, "Sorry if I sound like a doctor, but what seems to be the problem?"

"Well... there's this guy called Pimple... Billy Dinglefitz... and he's sort of, um, bullying me."

"Oh, dear, and do you have any idea why Billy is bothering you?"

"No. I honestly have no idea! I never did anything to him!"

"Well, if I asked you how do you think you could take control of the situation, would you have any ideas?"

Matt thought about the question for a while. "I don't know. They think I'm a coward, but if I fight back... well, they'll trash me. If I had already tried, you'd be talking to a big bowl of Matt-Mash!"

"That's not what I meant. But have you tried to get your friends to help?

Matt looked at his feet. "No-one wants to be my friend. They're afraid that they'll get hurt if they hang with me, maybe. But it's okay. I'm used to it."

"So Matt, how do you feel about being here?"

Matt stared at her and suddenly realised exactly how he felt. The realisation was so sudden and so plain that tears started holding a marathon on his cheeks.

"I... I wish I wasn't here!"

He started sobbing, the sorrow that he had been holding in for so long exploding out of him in one massive wave of sadness.

Caroline asked gently, "But Matt, what do you..."

"My dad died," Matt interrupted, "He died when I was five years old. I was still only a little kid. He's been gone forever, and I wish I was with him!"

The pain of loss wracked his body, gripping his heart in a vice of grief. Caroline gave him a tissue. "It's alright, Matt. So you miss your father?"

"Y-yes... I met someone who told me he was alive. An old lady. And there was a note. And my mother won't talk about it. Now I don't know what's real and what isn't anymore," he said, trying to speak through the sobbing, his head lowered to the table.

"Matt, when you feel saddest, like right now, just think about the best memories you have of him. Have you got one, right now, in your head? What is it?"

Very slowly Matt sat upright again.

"The... the day he carved all our names on the oak tree back home. It was the best day of my life..." He began to feel a little better.

Caroline smiled at him, giving him time to dwell on the memory.

Matt continued, "Every time anyone, you know, my mother or whoever, asked me to pray, I would always pray to my father. In primary school we were told that we had a guardian angel. I always picked him, my dad, to be my guardian angel. I prayed to him every night before I went to sleep... but maybe that didn't do me any good. I don't really know. If he is alive then why has he forgotten us?"

Matt was aware of the awful sadness in his voice. He hung his head again, staring at his shoes.

Gently, Caroline handed him a sheet of paper.

"Matt, it has been really nice meeting you. I feel so privileged that you have shared those private thoughts with me. And I assure you that they are private. You can come and talk to me anytime you like, but for now, Matt, I want you to fill out this exercise over the week. It's a list of things that might bother you. Just tick them if they do. Will you do that for me? And remember, I will only ever discuss any of your business with your principal and your mother if you are happy for me to do so."

"Okay," agreed Matt, wiping away his tears. "He took the paper, got to his feet and made for the door.

"Matt?" she said, just as his hand was touching the handle.

"Yeah?"

"When I can, I'll have a chat with your mother. Remember that what you shared with me is private. Between now and when we talk again, I want you to reach out to those you trust. Let someone know about this and above all, remember that it's not your fault. None of what has happened, including your run in with Billy, is your fault."

Silence reigned for a few seconds.

"Thank you, Caroline. You've really helped me today."

And he was gone.

- 7 -

RACHEL MEETS FRECKLES

Matt's slippered feet made no sound on the usually creaky, wooden floorboards of the hallway. He could hear Rachel talking on her phone in the kitchen.

"Yeah, got it Sandy. After swim session. Love to. Bye."

The beep meant she had hung up. Matt shuffled through the open door. Rachel was standing with her back to him. He took a deep breath. This was it, the moment of truth.

"Hiya."

Rachel shrieked and jumped a foot in the air, spinning as she went and almost landing on her butt, before she managed to steady herself.

Ah, back to normal, thanks to me, Matt thought.

"Jeez Matt, what are you, some kind of stalker?"

"No. I was just walking."

"You should wear a cowbell around your neck!"

"Listen Rachel! For once in your life, listen. I want to talk to you, okay?"

She calmed down and hoisted herself up onto her feet.

"Well?"

Matt took a deep breath.

"You know the dummy?"

"Well, duh!"

"Um, well, I can talk to it in my head sort of... "

"Yeah right," laughed Rachel, "and I'm married to Brian O'Driscoll. Get a life, Matt."

"I'm serious" Matt yelled. "It speaks to me as a voice in my freakin' head!"

Too late, Matt realised how crazy that sounded.

"A voice? In your head?" Rachel's eyes grew wide. "Now it's finally confirmed... you are delusional. Did that bang on the head knock out the last few brain cells you possessed?"

"Never mind. Forget I said anything."

Matt decided to go out for a stroll around the estate. He stomped upstairs to his bedroom to get his shoes.

"Stupid Rachel!" he muttered as he threw himself down into a tattered blue armchair in his room and began to pull on his trainers. "One minute she's nice and the next she's... she's Rachel."

Is she not taking the news very well? Mr Freckles asked.

Matt made a face. "She is not taking the news at all! She keeps saying you're just a stupid old dummy and I need a psychologist."

Mr Freckles was shocked. *She... she is making me out to be some sort of an uneducated ragamuffin!*

"I know. Sometimes she's a sorry excuse for a sister."

Never, not once in all my time in your family, have I been mocked – and that's a long time. Why, I have been with the O'Connors so long that I have forgotten my second name! It was probably something nice and sophisticated, such as Smyth or Nobel or Lindbergh or something of equal grace. My family came from a long line of lords and ladies you know. Speaking of that name, Lindbergh, did I ever tell you about the time your ancestor and I went to Paris to see Mr Lindbergh flying in from America, a great to-do altogether. We got to meet him, and I actually performed for him...

"Oi, Freckles, we're getting off track here."

Ahhh yes, wait, where were we?

"Rachel!"

Ohh, don't you worry, leave her to me. Just bring me to the kitchen on your way out, and seat me somewhere comfortable.

Matt did as the dummy had asked and then headed for the front door.

"I'm going out for a while," he shouted up the stairs, but Rachel was already on her way down.

"Yeah, yeah, whatever. No need to tell the whole world."

When Rachel entered the kitchen, she immediately spotted the dummy, which was propped up on the counter beside the fridge.

"Matt," she called, hoping to catch him before he left, "you left your little buddy behind you".

The sarcasm of the remark was lost on the banging door. As she strolled over to stare at the contents, or lack of, in the fridge, Rachel threw a sideways remark at Mr Freckles.

"So then, your minder forgot you, huh? Well, you can make your own way back."

Rachel took two slices of bread out of the cupboard. She scraped the mould off and placed them in the toaster. While she was waiting for them to pop up, she caught Mr Freckles' eye. It seemed to be staring at her.

"Don't look at me like that, you wooden freak!" She threw a tea towel over his face. "Wa... wait, did you just move?"

While Rachel stared at the crooked, slouching figure, ridiculous now, with its sheik-like appearance, the thick round breadboard suddenly toppled out from behind a set of knives and knocked over a cheap bottle of wine. Red wine spilled over the countertop and dripped down the side of the presses, landing at Rachel's feet. She stared in astonishment at it for a few seconds.

"Was that you?"

The whisper had barely escaped her lips when she looked down at the floor and was shocked into silence. The wine at her feet had pooled in a shape, the shape of a question mark. Rachel stumbled back against the counter, grabbing it with both hands to steady herself. She gasped for breath and then grabbed a few sheets of kitchen paper to mop up the mess. Red wine seeped into the ends of her soft pink sleeves, making it look as though they were drenched in blood.

"But... how?"

Rachel was shaking as she focused on the dummy. The tea towel slid off Mr Freckles' face to reveal a creepy smile.

His smug eyes appeared to stare straight into Rachel's. Rachel pinched herself. No... it wasn't a dream. She ran upstairs and knocked on her mother's bedroom door.

"Mum!"

"Come in Rach," replied a faint voice.

Rachel went in and approached the bed where her mother was lying. The floorboards groaned with every step she took.

"How are you? I brought hot chocolate, the end of the tin."

"Thanks, I don't know what I'd do without you," Colette replied. "I'm awfully tired today. I don't know why. It must have been the stress of the hospital."

Not sure how to broach the subject, Rachel thought it best just to come out and say it. "Mum, do you know the dummy Matt keeps in his room, the one with the funny hat he had as a baby? I think there's something weird about it." Rachel summoned all her courage before continuing, "I actually think it tried to talk to me!"

"What do you mean?"

"Well, I was in the kitchen, and it was sitting on the counter, just where Matt was not supposed to leave it. And I thought I saw it move. So I asked myself, did that dummy just move? Then, all of a sudden, the chopping board slid from where it was leaning near the draining board and knocked over that bottle of wine Ricky gave you. It broke, and the wine splashed all over the floor. When I leaned down to wipe it up, I saw that the wine had landed on the floor in the shape of a big question mark." Rachel took a deep breath, and her mother sighed.

"Oh Rach."

"Mum, you know I'd be the last person in the world to believe in stupid hocus pocus, but do you think it was a coincidence or did it try to... well... to communicate with me?"

There was silence.

"Well?" said Rachel impatiently. "Oh my God, Mum! I've just realised something. That must be who I hear Matt talking to. It all fits!"

"Oh dear," Colette closed her eyes. "Rachel, it's a dummy. Its name is Mr Tickles or whatever he's calling it now. Dummies don't talk, or communicate in any other way. You're imagining all this! The chopping board just slid on the wet surface. I can't begin to work out where he resurrected the hideous thing from. I thought it had gone up in the flames. Although, I can guess. I expressly forbade him from going anywhere near the wretched place and he does, and ends up in hospital. We're lucky he wasn't killed. He just can't go there again."

"Why not?"

"You know why not."

Rachel persisted, despite the risk that her mother would retreat into her usual silence.

"Mum, Matt is a boy. He wants to explore the place where he lived when he was small. You need to explain to him what happened back there."

The remark had the feared effect. Colette lay back down on the pillow with a groan.

"Rachel, love, you know our agreement. I won't have Matt going near that place. There are holes, and the stable roofs could collapse. He could hurt himself and we wouldn't even know. I need to give him a good talking to."

Colette closed her eyes.

There was silence for several moments. Rachel noticed a spider climbing up the wall behind her mother's bed.

"We'll have to give the house a good clean one of the days," she commented.

There was no response.

"Mum," Rachel went on, "do you think Dad will come back?"

Colette's eyes briefly opened

"Oh my, look at the time," she said. "You had better hop off to bed or you won't get up for school in the morning!"

Realising that her mother was deliberately ignoring the question, Rachel gave her a small hug and went to her own bedroom, worrying about the lack of food and whether there would be enough for breakfast.

- 8 -

THE PRANK

I t was Friday, and Matt had spent every moment since a minute past five looking out of the window. He had tried to tell his mother that he was having a guest over for a few games, but he wasn't sure that the message had sunk in. Concerned that David's mother would come into the house, Matt was hoping that his mother would be out of bed and dressed by the time his friend arrived. This was looking less likely as the evening wore on.

Rachel promised Matt that she would meet David's mother if she came to the door. She approved of her brother's new friend but stopped way short of a public introduction in school, growling side-mouthed at Matt not to push it when he had offered. Now she was busy about the kitchen, trying to scramble together the last few bits of edible material into something resembling a decent meal. She found a bag of potatoes in the cupboard. They would just about do, accompanied by some frozen Chicken Kiev she had found languishing at the bottom of the freezer. The table was set for four, even though they both knew that one plate of food would be placed in the oven to be transferred upstairs when Colette was up to eating it.

As soon as the doorbell rang, Matt stuffed Mr Freckles into the wardrobe and went downstairs to join Rachel at the door. David was standing on the doorstep with his young, confident-looking mother. As Matt and David bounded up the stairs, Matt could hear his sister explaining that Colette was having a nap and conveying apologies on her behalf. Before closing the door, Rachel assured David's mother that they would take good care of her son.

Later on, happily sated by their dinner, the boys played games for a while and were then summoned to help Rachel with the washing up. This wasn't up for negotiation, and Matt was sharply put in his place when he suggested that their guest shouldn't have to work.

"If he eats, he washes up," Rachel dictated.

Her tone was cutting, bringing a finality that wasn't to be trifled with. The boys worked silently and speedily, Matt clearing the washed up dishes as David dried them.

"Your sister is a little bit bossy, I don't like her very much," David remarked when they were safely upstairs again.

"Me neither. That was nothing. You should see her when she goes properly bonkers... on second thoughts maybe you shouldn't. You'd be scarred for life."

"Is she hard to live with?"

"Hard to live with? Sometimes it's like living with an alien... teenage sisters are a different species. She can turn completely savage when there's a full moon and lots of other times too for no reason at all, if you get my drift."

"Yeah, don't even go there. My older brother too, he completely blanks me sometimes and when mum and dad don't give him what he wants, he seems to take it out on yours truly."

"What a cruel world we live in," Matt laughed.

"I don't let him get away with it, though."

"What do you do?"

"Pranks. They are the answer. Carefully thought out and meticulously planned practical jokes that get the older brother in trouble with the parents and give the younger sibling the most satisfaction," David explained in a phoney Australian accent. "You should try it sometime, mate... but not when I'm around, d'ya folla?"

Their conversation was interrupted by the sound of a car horn, gently reminding them that it was time for David to leave. Matt saw him out. David's mother gave him a friendly wave and a smile. It lit up the dreariness of the wet and windy evening and took his mind off the neglected homework that still needed his attention.

***

In the darkness of the wardrobe, Mr Freckles was dreaming about his earliest days with Matt's great, great grandfather; that black sheep of the O'Connor family, Charles O'Connor. Thoughts of those magical theatrical performances of the early 20th century came flooding back. That had been when the awareness first came.

Charles O'Connor was by no means the world's greatest ventriloquist; but it must have been the constant yearning for perfection, the incessant pressure to move his wooden body in harmony with his master, which caused Mr Freckles to tune into his practical jokes, his mannerisms and, eventually, his thoughts.

As he waited for young Matt to finish dining with his new friend, Mr Freckles enjoyed his sentimentalising. It was when his first master, Charles, took to the whiskey in his later years, "to relieve the loneliness of genius," as he put it, that he began to treat Mr Freckles as an equal, a companion, a friend. With these long, late nights and many slurred conversations, the understanding eventually came. And yet despite his mastering of the English language, Mr Freckles could never master the art of actual speech. He was equipped with no greater speaking tools than a double-hinged mouth and rigid red lips over a square chin, but he possessed nothing that could be persuaded to pump air through his nostrils or mouth.

But he could control his eyes. His master had always reassured him with that hackneyed phrase of his, "the eyes are the windows of the soul," as if it were possible for a wooden dummy to possess such a thing as a soul. He must now subdue these same black, all-seeing eyes if he were to avoid sending young Matt straight to the asylum for the insane.

But the time for action, and drastic action at that, was upon them now. Richard Moseley was evil, Mr Freckles knew, and he needed to thwart him and his powerful allies through the actions of twelve-year-old Matt. If urgent measures were not taken, Matt's family would be destroyed and neither his father nor the treasure he protected would ever be seen again.

But how could Mr Freckles train the child to communicate with him without driving him insane? He had learned to control electricity and the contraptions that depended on it for their life force, but he figured he would have to gain mastery of that infernal tool that Matt called his Peecee, if any progress was to be made in the lingo department. Mr Freckles realised that he would need to be cautious - the Peecee was the same device Moseley apparently used to communicate with Matt - but it was vital that he learn to use this wretched monstrosity to speak to the lad.

Mr Freckles was interrupted by the door opening. Matt lifted him out of the wardrobe.

What a rude interruption, old boy! I was having a lovely dream, about myself.

"Maybe I should prank Rachel? What do you think?" Matt asked.

Well, she is always bothering you. Perhaps it is high time you gave her a bit of a jolt, just to show her that you actually exist, old chap, if that really is your pleasure?

It may have been a figment of his imagination, but he could have sworn he saw the dummy's mouth move yet again.

"Old chap? Who are you calling old? Do you actually speak or do we have some sort of telepathic connection?" Matt said playfully.

Wouldn't you like to know?

"Yes, I would like to know."

Matt looked thoughtfully at the dummy.

I will, I won't, I will, I won't, the words bounced back and forth in his mind like a tennis ball on an especially springy court.

"You know what," he said eventually, "I will do it! She annoys me, so I'll annoy her. But what should I do?"

An idea sprang into his mind. "You thinking what I'm thinking?" he asked Mr Freckles.

Yes. But no, that certainly is not advisable, the dummy answered.

"Shower or wardrobe?"

Don't you think I am a little too old to be in a young lady's bedroom?

"How old are you anyway?"

Somewhere in the region of two hundred, give or take a few decades.

"C'mon, Rachel hates you. It'll be perfect!"

I agree then! But not the... what did you call it... the shower. I respect your sister's privacy and to be quite frank, I have no wish to be there. And let it be noted for the record that I am distinctly uncomfortable with this prank proposal.

"So we really are communicating with one another. This is awesome. I must start practising my ventriloquistical skills... if that's a word."

It isn't.

"Fair enough. Maybe I'll just use you in Halloween shows. I guess I'll have to start practising my evil laugh. Mwa ha ha ha," Matt cut off, coughing. "Don't worry, I'll keep practising," he gasped, reaching for his blue inhaler.

You do that.

Half an hour later, Matt was crouched down in front of Rachel's bedroom door, peering through the keyhole. The dummy was in Rachel's wardrobe, where he had been placed leaning against the door in a standing position, his leering grin waiting for Rachel. Matt heard the water being turned off in the shower of the en-suite bathroom.

Perfect. Now all I have to do is wait for the fun to begin, he thought.

Rachel stepped out of her bathroom, clutching a towel around her. She walked over to the wardrobe and opened the door, but the sight that met her eyes was not that of her carefully arranged clothes, but the hideous, grotesque dummy that her brother had dragged home. She screamed in fright, lifting both hands to her head and dropping her towel in the process.

Matt averted his eyes. Gross. He waited until he thought Rachel

was decent before looking through the keyhole again. Fully clothed now, Rachel stormed to the door and opened it, a furious expression on her face.

"Matthew O'Connor!" she screamed, "you stupid little pig! That dummy's dead!"

Rachel went back into her room, picked up Mr Freckles and threw him out of the window.

"You idiot!" Matt shouted, with a rare burst of confidence.

He bounded down the stairs, taking them three steps at a time and ran out of the front door. Mr Freckles lay in mangled pieces on the ground. Matt gathered all the pieces together and brought them up to his bedroom. He tried intently to put them back together. It was no use. He could fit an arm into its socket here, two fingers in a hand there, but when it came to putting all the parts together, the whole thing just fell apart.

"Aaarghhh!" He threw the pieces to the floor in frustration.

With the rush of adrenalin that had flowed through his veins all but gone, Matt began to tremble. He flung himself face-down on the bed and cried, his mysterious burst of confidence vanishing into thin air.

Everything good seemed to have been taken away from him; his Dad, who had been his best friend, was gone; his mum had disappeared into the shadowy, dark world to which her mood and medication had condemned her; even Rachel had been moderately nice to him before his father disappeared; and now Mr Freckles was no more than a pile of wooden pieces.

He hem.

Matt heard what he thought was a little cough. He turned over onto his side, sniffling. He looked over, and there sitting in its usual spot in the corner, was his old friend, fully intact.

I'm scarred for life, announced Mr Freckles.

Matt laughed.

- 9 -

TROUBLE FOR RACHEL

Food is running out, thought Rachel, as she poured the last few bits of cereal into a bowl, *and we've barely any money to buy more.*

Money had been plentiful before their father had disappeared. Ronan had a good job working in the Department of Agriculture, among other things. Colette had worked as a dental assistant before she became depressed, when everyone finally gave up on ever finding Ronan again. The house was now covered in a layer of dust that nobody would clean.

Rachel strolled over to the fridge and took out the last litre of milk. There was only half of it left, and it was already out of date. On the first sniff, it seemed passable, but it didn't look good when poured over the cereal and tasted much worse than it smelled. *It will have to do*, she thought.

"Matt," she called, "I'm going shopping. You can have the cereal on the table. I poured out some, but I don't feel hungry any more. Don't let it go to waste."

Really? Thought Matt, as he ran down the stairs. *Rachel doing something nice for me, Matthew O'Connor?*

Matt sat down at the table in the corner where his sister had left the cereal. He picked up a spoon and began to stuff it into his mouth before the sickening tang of the sour milk assaulted his taste buds. He gagged and almost threw up, spitting the food back into the bowl.

"Rachel!" he shouted with a touch of anger, "This milk is sour!" *I just knew there was a catch,* he thought.

"I know," came the reply. "I'll be back in ten, maybe less if I can't afford anything."

Rachel locked the door behind her on the way out. Hanging her mum's large, worn handbag and a shopping bag over the handlebars, she jumped on her bike and cycled off.

As soon as she got to the supermarket, Rachel tied her bike to a metal bar outside. She couldn't afford a lock, but she thought to herself, *who would want this wreck of a bike anyway?* Walking through the automatic doors, she made her way to the dairy aisle, making sure to check the price of the milk before buying. *Two euro fifty for two litres – what a rip-off! I can only afford to spend a fiver today at the rate we're going.* This was when the idea struck her. Would she? Wouldn't she? How easy it would be to slip a few things under her jacket without anyone noticing.

Rachel was aware of the little black bubble-like cameras that could see in all directions, but then, what good are cameras if no one is watching through them?

Rachel ambled over to the little booth just inside the front door where the security guard usually sat staring at the monitor. It was unmanned.

It's now or never, she thought, as she walked confidently back to the dairy section.

At the end of the aisle was a small stand that displayed little containers of yoghurt. Rachel casually strolled past, grabbed a carton with the tips of her fingers and discreetly stowed it in her shopping basket, intending to find a better hiding place before she left. A pleasant young woman approached the stand and began smiling. *Drat it, she's on to me.*

"Hello there. Did you know you can get two for the price of one?" the young lady asked.

Rachel jumped, almost wetting herself with fear, but then she saw the sign that told her that the cartons were on promotion.

"Oh, err... yes please!"

The woman explained about all the different flavours and the special offer. Rachel felt obliged to have a taste of almost every single one before she could return to the milk counter. *I've got three mouths to feed*, she thought, *and I can't come back until tomorrow. So I have to get breakfast, lunch and dinner.*

The 500ml cartons of milk were too bulky to fit under her coat, so Rachel slipped two of them into her handbag. Then, she cautiously walked out of the shop, put the milk into her shopping bag and placed the bag into the basket of her bike.

That was easy, she thought. *I think I'll get some more.*

She returned to the shop, braver now. A quick check of the security box told her it was still empty. She pulled her hood up and walked with renewed confidence to the furthest end of the shop.

Rachel quickly pilfered a small box of cereal, especially for Matt, and a packet of crisps. Then she went to the frozen foods section to see if there was a pizza small enough to fit in her bag. She looked at them for a moment before deciding to get three mini ones instead. She was about to nab them when an old lady walked up the aisle. Her eyes quickly swept over Rachel before she began to question her in a kind-old-lady-not-trying-to-accuse-you-of-anything voice.

"Are you okay there, dear?"

"Fine, just picking up a couple of pizzas. You know us teenagers, always living on pizzas and fries."

Rachel slowly sauntered towards the check-outs.

I think I'll buy the pizzas, she thought. *I have enough money, and it will cause less suspicion.*

The three people queuing ahead of her seemed to take forever. When it was finally her turn, Rachel peeled back her hood and placed the pizzas on the belt.

"Hello," said the lady at the counter.

"Hi," answered, Rachel, surprising even herself with the confidence in her own voice.

"How are you?"

"Great, thank you."

"Is that everything?" the lady asked, a little too slowly. Rachel nodded.

"That'll be three-ninety-nine please."

Rachel handed over the five-euro note.

"Thank you," said the cashier. "Here's your change. You have a good night."

In her rush to get away, Rachel almost forgot to take the change. When she remembered, she mustered enough composure to smile at the cashier before making her way increasingly rapidly to the exit and her bike. She couldn't help but feel eyes on the back of her head, as she began to ride slowly away. *Stop imagining things. You're free and clear, girl.*

To her horror, she heard a man's voice calling after her.

"Young lady. Hey young lady! One moment please. You there! Hold on a minute."

Rachel could hear someone running behind her, but she could not allow herself to be caught. Her bike found a speed that it never knew before as she dodged in front of a skidding car to escape her pursuer.

When she reached her home, Rachel slammed the door behind her.

Whew! That was close, she thought.

An hour later, the three pizzas were cooking, alongside some oven chips, when there was a knock at the door.

Rachel's heart raced and skipped a few beats. She slowly approached the door and opened it. A man, wearing a shirt from the store she'd just visited, was standing on her doorstep. He was accompanied by a member of the Garda Síochána. In the street outside, a police car sat purring patiently.

Rachel stared at them blankly.

"Who is it?" Matt shouted from the sitting room, where he was watching television.

"Oh, just Derek," Rachel called, closing the sitting room door.

"Miss," began the Garda, "this man here is the manager at a local supermarket. He has informed me that someone stole food and drink from his shop. He tried calling the thief back, but she did not respond. He followed her here in his car and then called us. He says that the alleged thief entered this house and looks very like you. In fact, we believe it was you."

"I... I didn't steal anything. I wasn't shopping today."

"Miss, it was caught on camera, so unless you have a twin or someone virtually identical to you, you have been stealing!"

"I... but..." Rachel stammered.

The Garda picked up a receipt from where it was lying on the counter top, read the date and looked at Rachel with a raised eyebrow.

"So you weren't shopping today?" she said. "Then who bought these groceries? Are your parents here?"

"No. There is no-one here but me and my brother, Matt. He's watching TV in the living room. Neither of my parents are home."

"I am going to have to talk to one of them before we proceed further with this. For now, I will simply ask that you come clean, tell me your name and age and admit that you were in the store at 11 a.m."

The young Garda was calm, almost kind, as if she felt sorry for Rachel.

"It's obvious that you made these purchases, but you picked up some special offers too, didn't you?" she said. "I'm sorry, but we will have to either speak with your parents or bring you back to the shop, where we can talk things over in more detail."

"You can't prove I stole anything!"

"They have caught you on camera. How old are you?"

"Eighteen."

The Garda conferred with the store manager before turning again to Rachel.

"Now Miss, we really will have to talk to your mother or father."

Rachel shook her head without saying anything.

The Garda filled the silence. "If they're not available, you'll have to come with us."

Rachel reluctantly followed the Garda into the squad car.

When they arrived at the supermarket, the Garda and the manager brought Rachel to a small room near the back of the shop.

"You may take a seat," the manager said. He switched on a computer monitor on the metal desk nearby and pulled up video footage of the shop floor.

Rachel collapsed onto one of the chairs that stood either side of the desk. The room was small and dark, with a gloomy, cloistered feel. There were no windows, just one small vent in the wall, and the naked bulb that hung unadorned from the low ceiling gave out little light. There were a few untidy shelves and a stack of plastic, grey chairs in one corner.

This must be the torture room, Rachel considered, but decided to keep the remark to herself. *I won't give them ideas.*

"Now," began the Garda, "what's your name?"

"Louise Evans," Rachel's answer was automatic and just a little too prepared.

"Are you sure?" asked the Garda. There is no Louise Evans at the address we just visited. I believe it's the O'Connors who live there. We are trying to reach your mother at the moment, but she doesn't appear to be answering her phone. Are you sure she's at work?"

"Yes," said Rachel, with just hint of a nervous smirk on her lips. She was never good at lying.

The manager pressed a button, and footage of Rachel walking along the supermarket aisles appeared on the screen.

The next question from the officer was much more insistent.

"All right, young lady. You've wasted too much of our time. The truth now, please."

"Alright, alright. I'm Rachel O'Connor. And I'm fifteen. Okay?"

"Less of the attitude, Rachel O'Connor. And do you, or do you not, live at No. 9 Forest View, Tullamore?"

"I do." Now that her flimsy cover had been abandoned, Rachel felt somewhat relieved.

"And you admit that you stole from this store earlier?" The manager swung the monitor around so that she could clearly see herself in the video footage, placing items under her clothes.

"I... but... um."

"Yes or no?" asked the Garda, pointing at the footage.

"Yes! Now, are you happy? There, I admit it. Yes, that was me. Is me."

"I don't understand. Why did you steal?" added the Garda.

"Because we didn't have enough money for your stupid, expensive milk," said Rachel, eyeing the young store manager.

"Did your parents know you were at the store?"

"It's my fault, not theirs. I should have had more sense," Rachel answered weakly.

"And your parents knew you were shopping? What would they say if they were looking at this video of you, as we are now?" asked the Guard.

"Well, my Dad's dead. And I have to look after things at home. As for my mother, if you must know, I don't think she would really care."

The statement brought a temporary halt to the flow of questioning.

"Really, why wouldn't she care?" said the policewoman eventually.

"Well, ever since my Dad died... " Rachel faltered, dropping her head into her hands. "My Mum's depressed... okay?" She broke down now, trying to stifle the sobs that welled up, despite her best efforts to subdue them.

"But surely you didn't have to steal. Is there no one to help you out?"

"No, there's only my younger brother Matt and me. And quite simply, we have no money."

As she dialled a number on her phone, the Garda kept glancing at Rachel.

"How come your mother won't answer? Is she normally this hard to reach?"

"Yes. And you'll be lucky if you ever get through to her. There's just me and my brother really. She takes these pills called Prozac, three times a day, and by now, she will be well and truly out for the count."

"Three times a day?" The Garda gave Rachel an odd look. "Who is her doctor?"

"I don't know. Mum's pharmacist said to have it with every meal, but there's something fishy about him... I know there is. He stopped her going to the doctor. He brings the stuff round himself."

"So you have a suspect pharmacist, and your mum doesn't take care of you?"

"Ah, yes, and no."

"Who does then?"

"I'm well capable of taking care of myself!"

Rachel felt indignant now despite the kindness of her questioner. Maybe this young policewoman might be able to help. She might reopen the case of her missing father or bring back the mother Rachel had known. But Rachel had been worn down since the raid all those years ago; the-long-drawn-out investigation, the suspicion, the looks from the mean kids at school, and the years of watching her mother wither and turn into a zombie edition of her former self. Her trust in the justice system and the power of the police was well and truly shattered. She wouldn't go back there again.

"Right then, we had better get you home now. Mr Mason, could you please escort Miss O'Connor out to the car while I make a phone call?" asked the Garda.

"Of course," replied the store manager, giving Rachel a sympathetic look. This hurt more than anger would have. The man opened the door politely and accompanied her to the waiting police car.

By the time they arrived back at the house, someone else was standing on the doorstep. Tall and skinny, he had black hair and was wearing a black two-piece suit. The look was somewhat softened by the ponytail hanging down his back.

"So this is the right place then?" he asked.

"Yes," said the Garda.

"Who is he?" asked Rachel, with a touch of fear in her voice. "And what's he doing here?"

"I am John Flanagan," he said. "I work for the Social Services." He had a pleasant, positive manner about him.

They went inside.

"Now, Miss O'Connor," said Flanagan, "would you get your mother please?"

The policewoman and the social worker stood at the bottom of the stairs while Rachel half walked, half stumbled up to her mother's bedroom and turned on the light.

"What is it?" Colette mumbled. "Turn that light off please."

"Mrs O'Connor," John called from downstairs. "I am John Flanagan, social worker with the HSE. Your daughter has gotten herself into a spot of bother, and we need to talk to you. Can you come downstairs please?"

Colette shielded her eyes from the overhead light.

"Rachel, are you there love? What's all this? Who is that?" The voice that came from the bundle of bedclothes was weak, vulnerable.

"Mum, these people have to speak to you. They need you to come downstairs. You'll have to get dressed and come down." Rachel's tone was plaintive and tender towards her mother but not so when she turned and called sharply downstairs. "Can you give us a minute please, my mother would like to get dressed first, if you don't mind?"

Disturbed by the voices, Matt came out of his bedroom, where he had been playing on his computer.

"Matt!" Rachel barked at him, "I need you to put the kettle on and make some tea for everyone. We have guests, the police, in case you hadn't noticed. There's milk in the fridge."

Rachel didn't hear the voice that echoed in Matt's head as he made his way down the stairs.

You have to step up, Matthew. Your sister is a minor. She cannot be arrested or placed in a penitentiary. You have to make good her mistake. Take charge of the situation.

Matt pondered this strange advice from Mr Freckles as he put the teabags into the pot.

Five minutes later, everyone was sitting awkwardly in the sitting room, sipping the overly strong tea Matt had made, awkwardly waiting for someone to begin speaking. Colette was the last person to take her seat, patiently helped by her daughter.

"Mrs O'Connor," began the man with the ponytail, "I am John Flanagan from Midland Social Services, and I am here on foot of a complaint of neglect made against you by An Garda Síochána and an accusation of theft against your daughter."

The statement hung in the air of its own absurdity in the dark sitting room. Matt gasped, and Rachel stared disbelievingly at the female officer on whom she had earlier pinned just a small grain of hope, realising that the hope was poorly founded. The Garda would not meet her eyes.

The social worker continued. "It's all very simple, Mrs O'Connor. Once we have been informed that you are not taking proper care of your children, and that they have had to fend for themselves, it is incumbent on us to take action. Your daughter here was caught stealing this afternoon."

"What are you saying? I don't understand." Colette reeled in disbelief. "Rachel, love, why would you do such a thing?"

"Because we've no money to buy anything with! If you'd get yourself out of bed and get a job, or your old one back, we might be able to live a nice life."

"Don't speak to Mum like that!" Matt said.

"Thank you," said Colette to Matt, before turning to the adults. "Could you please let us sort this out among ourselves? I'm sure there's been some misunderstanding."

"Sorry, Mrs O'Connor, but once we have a report of neglect or where children are in danger and a crime is committed, we are involved. You're not doing right by your children from what we've been told. It appears that you are incapable of getting out of bed to take care of your family. If you are unwell, we can get help for you. That's why we're here," said Flanagan.

"It's not her fault if she's depressed." The sudden strength and forcefulness in Matt's voice took everyone by surprise. "We've enough money to buy groceries, and we are more than happy to pay for whatever Rachel took. We can make it right, can't we Rachel?"

"It mightn't be as simple as that," the policewoman interjected, "if the shop presses charges."

Matt cut her off, speaking in authoritative tones on behalf of his family.

"As soon as you leave our house, the three of us are going to go down there to pay them for the cereal, crisps and milk. My sister is fifteen; if they want to put her in jail on account of a stupid mistake, that's their business, but we know what we have to do to make this right, and we'll do it."

Rachel gave her brother a look of utter disbelief. From the downtrodden victim of school bullies to her knight in shining armour... almost. She held back a sisterly smile... now wasn't the time. Perhaps some waterworks might be in order, she thought, before allowing the pressure she had been feeling all along to overcome her. She opened up the flood gates.

"My brother is right," she sobbed. "I'm really sorry I took those groceries. I thought it would be a dare, but I didn't realise the trouble I'd cause. I'm sorry, Mum, I really shouldn't have said what I did just now. I really was wrong. And I am sorry for wasting everyone's time." She moved over closer to her mother, who put her arm around her daughter's shoulders.

Rachel felt a support and warmth from her mother she had almost forgotten existed and responded with a hug of her own. Her tears were now for real. Through the blurred corner of her eye, she noticed Matt and wanted to hug him too. *How was he so brave?* she wondered. But her brother looked quite content, almost detached and oblivious.

The Garda stood up. "I'll go for now. I will be in contact if the supermarket decides to press charges."

The social worker followed her lead. "There are quite a few unresolved issues outstanding, Mrs O'Connor," he said before he left. "I will have to call back in a day or two to follow up on them, talk to your doctor and so on. For now, I wish you well."

Once Matt had seen the visitors out, the warm, supportive atmosphere rapidly vanished. As the cars pulled away from the driveway, he could hear the voices in the sitting room growing louder and angrier. By the time he re-entered, the shouting had started.

"Rachel, why would you steal? How could you do that to us?"

"Because I didn't want to go hungry, and maybe if you tried to help, you know, got up out of that bed, got your job back, we might be able to make some money... just enough to live on like everybody else," Rachel retorted, her voice trailing off. The accusation was hard for her.

"Hey, I thought we were done with all that", Matt chirped from the doorway. "Now if you two can pull yourselves together, we need to get down to the shop and pay our family debts. All of us. What do you girls think?"

The unexpected strength in her son's voice seemed to rouse Colette from her usual stupor.

"I'll get my coat," she said, "and we'll go together".

- 10 -

PROZAC

Durrow Abbey. The sounds of gunshots rang out through the rough greenery and leafy branches. Ronan O'Connor kissed his two young children and faced his wife. "Colette," he said, "be strong. You know what I must do. I love you". Then he gently pushed her towards the trapdoor into which he had just lowered the children. "They need you."

Someone was shouting. It was Mr Freckles, but the words were lost in the wind.

Matt woke up with a start. It was evening, and he was slumped over his desk, where he remembered sitting sometime earlier and beginning his homework. He felt dizzy, and his forehead was damp and clammy.

"What... on... Earth." Matt knew his dream had meant something, but what?

Ehh... a voice said in Matt's head.

"Mr Freckles?" Matt was getting used to hearing the dummy's voice in his head, but it still made him jump.

Yes Matthew, it is I. I am slightly concerned for you, old boy.

"I'm fine. Are you alright?"

Just about. Putting a dream inside the head of a very deep sleeper is very, very mentally challenging!

"I didn't know I was a very deep sleeper. What were you doing putting a dream inside my head?"

Mr Freckles ignored the question.

On the day your father had to leave, you slept through the break in and only woke when your mother took you down the stairs, through the tunnel and out to the stables.

"Wait... you know? Were you there?"

I didn't say I was there, but did I not show you all that in your dream?

"Did you tell me it all? Is there more that I should know about?"

You will find out eventually, by yourself.

"Come on! I have to do everything myself! If you know something, please tell me."

I'm afraid I can't do that, Matthew.

"Well just tell me where my dad went then."

Sorry Matthew, but I can't. You have to discover some things yourself.

Matt switched on his computer and opened PenChat.

Please do not tell me that you intend to speak to that make-believe friend of yours.

"If you're not going to answer my questions, then just be quiet."

You mean for me to be silent.

"Exactly. Well done."

Matt logged into his account and skimmed the mouse across his colourfully decorated desktop. He had programmed all of 101's messages to flash red and blue if he hadn't checked them yet. His eyes lit up when he saw that there was a new one that had only been sent two minutes before. Matt clicked on it and smiled as he read the jumbled up message:

'Hey 102: How's things? Listen, I just got back from the cinema. I went to see *Correction: Time to Die* and it was brilliant. But it got me thinking about what 102's favourite film is? So, what is it buddy?'

Matt pressed reply with a smile on his face: 'Hi 101. In reply to your question, my most favourite film would have to be *Legend of Nikan*.'

'Last week my dad took me to see *Shooting of Elite 3*. It was great.'

Wow, he actually got to see that, Matt thought.

'That's so cool,' typed Matt. 'I love films, but I don't have enough money to go that often and that film you saw is rated 18, right?'

That Noname is no good. Something is not right about him, said Mr Freckles.

"You shut up and mind your own business," Matt fired back, a little too loudly.

You didn't tell me to shut up when I pointed out that the policeman could not arrest your sister.

Before Matt could reply, a small beep came from the computer, but Mr Freckles was on a roll.

Well, well. You tell me to "shut up," but do not do the same to that electronic brain. I think you have made it clear whom you favour.

Matt ignored his wooden friend and read Noname's message.

'Yeah, it is rated 18, but I got into it when the first one came out. Then, it was only rated 12. It's my favourite film series. What's yours?'

Matt didn't even have to think. As he typed in the answer, he thought of the money he had saved up to see the next film in his favourite trilogy. There was a lot less now, he thought, since he had acted the rich guy and paid for the items that his sister had... eh... ordered. The computer beeped again, and Matt eagerly opened the reply.

'I love going with my dad. Is that sister of yours still annoying you?'

'She's not too bad really, but she cost me a bunch of money a couple of days ago.'

'Whatcha mean?'

'She went on a little shopping trip to our local supermarket but forgot to pay for the stuff. I had to cough up to stop her getting in trouble. We had cops and social workers at our house. It was a mess.'

Matthew, you are telling the family business to a stranger. Have my cautions fallen completely on deaf ears? We shouldn't wash our dirty linen in public you know.

'Gotta go,' Matt typed, ignoring Mr Freckles. 'Rachel's calling me. Later dude.'

"Hey Matt," she said, bursting into his room and casting a nervous glance at the dummy.

"Put that... thing in the wardrobe, would you?" she asked.

Did Rachel just talk to me? Matt wondered, quickly turning off PenChat and removing Mr Freckles from view, *is she standing in my room?*

"Matt," said Rachel, "I need to talk to you about Mum".

"What's up with her now?" said Matt worriedly. "Is she getting worse?"

"I..." Rachel hesitated, "I have a bad feeling about those meds that she's supposed to be taking, Prozac. I looked it up, and you are only supposed to take it once a day, and visit your doctor about it regularly. She takes it with every meal, Matt, and besides us, the only person she talks to about her problems is that Ricky Moseley guy."

"He's a pharmacist or something," Matt reminded her.

"He's a delivery guy for a pharmacy, and a grocery store. And he's the one who told us that she had to take it with every meal, remember? I don't trust him. Besides we don't know he's actually a chemist or whatever he's supposed to be, do we?"

Matt thought for a moment. "Let me look him up on the Internet."

A brief search of pharmacists in the Tullamore area came up blank.

"So, if our delivery guy is just that, and not a medicine man of any kind, what do we do?"

"I don't know. I was hoping you might come up with something."

Matt thought for a while. Then an idea came from somewhere.

"How about we switch her Prozac for some of those vitamin C tablets? They look much the same. That might work."

"Matt, that's brilliant!" Rachel did a victory lap of the bedroom. "Okay, now then, truce over. Get back to your work, idiot!"

Matt could hear Rachel bounding down the stairs as he restored Mr Freckles to his rightful throne on the computer desk.

I never get the credit for anything, came the thought, loud and clear.

"I'd have a hard time explaining that one, now, wouldn't I?" Matt laughed.

An hour later, Matt was doing his homework when the doorbell rang.

Rachel, who had been sitting on the couch reading a magazine, was just getting up to answer the door when her mother appeared in the hallway, almost knocking her over.

"It's for me darling," said Colette, as she opened the door.

"Ricky!" she exclaimed, feigning surprise, "I thought you had too much work to do."

"I think I can spare enough time to take a special lady out for dinner," Moseley replied, giving her a kiss.

Behind their backs, Rachel mimed being sick.

"What is all the racket down here?" Matt asked, bounding down the stairs. "Oh, it's him," he added, exchanging a frown with Rachel.

"What was that darling?" Colette asked, not really paying attention.

"Nothing, Mum," Matt mumbled.

"I brought this for you two," Ricky interjected, holding out a DVD.

"Thanks," said Rachel, taking the gift.

"Aw... you're so sweet, bringing pressies for the kids," cooed Colette.

"We'd better go. I have the meal booked for seven at the Castle. We're running late already," said Ricky. "Bye Rochelle. See ya Matt."

"Rache..." she began to correct him, but the door shut before she could finish.

Colette and Ricky walked outside and got into a red convertible, which was parked in the driveway.

As they drove off, Rachel muttered, "Jerk couldn't even get my name right".

"But the DVD is *The Hobbit, An Unexpected Journey*. How did he know I loved that movie?" said Matt.

"Don't know. Maybe he's just your type," she teased.

"How did he get that, and it's only out in the cinema?"

"Who cares?"

"You wanna watch it with me?"

"I don't want anything to do with anything he touches. Besides, now would be a good time for us to put our cunning plan into action."

"If you mean exchange the contents of Mum's tablets, the only place open at this time of night is the supermarket. Are you sure you want to go back there?"

"I can walk in there holding my head up high thanks to my gallant brother. But, ah... hang on 'till I get my hoodie. Have you got any money left in that little stash of yours?"

"For this, yes," Matt said, running up the stairs.

***

Ricky Moseley and Colette drove up to one of the best restaurants in Tullamore. Colette admired the grand doors with their shining golden handles. *How can Ricky afford to bring me to such a fabulous place?* she wondered.

"So... what do you think?" Ricky asked Colette, as he pulled out a velvet chair for her.

"This restaurant is beautiful," Colette replied, her eyes sweeping across the ornately decorated walls and the richly carpeted floors.

"Only the best for you, my sweet," said Ricky. "I bet you haven't been to a place like this recently, have you?"

"Well when my husband was alive..." Colette began, but then realised what she was saying. "I mean, this is much better. Thank you so much for bringing me here. It must be quite expensive?"

Ricky smiled, "You are worth your weight, however light it may be, in gold."

Colette smiled at the compliment.

Ricky continued, "So, anyway, how have you been? Are you feeling alright?"

"Fine," she smiled.

A look of frustration flitted across Ricky's face, but before Colette could fully see what it was, it vanished.

"That's fantastic. The medication is working then? You've upped the dosage like I suggested?"

"Of course, but you're the only medicine I need. You give me an incentive to get out of bed every day. Well nearly every day." She stroked his hand across the table as she spoke. "So yes, you could say, working like a charm."

"I am glad," he said tenderly, but with a strange expression in his eyes, returning the touch and leaning in for a kiss. Just as their lips were about to touch, a waiter bustled over.

"Excuse me, are you ready to order?"

They both looked at the waiter in astonishment. They had completely forgotten where they were.

"Can we have a few more minutes please?" Colette requested.

The waiter was about to inform her that they had already been there for ten minutes, when he caught the look on Ricky's face, a look that he thought better than to argue with. He swallowed and hurried off.

Colette studied the menu, baffled at all the wonderful choices before her. She had never realised she could get such a wide selection of food for a single starter in just one restaurant, but finally she decided to go with her favourite: grilled swordfish with a small salad on the side.

Ricky summoned the waiter to their table with an imperious flick of the hand. The man left what he was doing and rushed over to them.

"What can I get you, madam?" he asked, choosing not to look at Ricky, who was persisting with his malevolent glare.

"I think I'll have the grilled swordfish and… "

Ricky interrupted before she could finish, "A bottle of your house red and we'll both have the Caesar salad, followed by the paella".

Colette was taken aback and sneaked a sideways glance at Ricky, but he ignored her.

"I just want you to keep your beautiful figure," he said, with his eyes still on the waiter as he handed him back the menus.

"How did you know what wine to order?" Colette asked.

"I know you like red, and this one is very good. And just trust me on the food. The paella is fantastic. Just as good as the Spanish stuff."

As the waiter was pouring their wine Ricky put his hand over his glass and said, "driving".

Colette smiled uncomfortably and stared down at her shoes.

While Colette and Ricky Moseley were out at the restaurant, Matt and Rachel put their plan into action. They made a quick dash to the shop to buy vitamin C tablets. When they got home, Rachel reached into the cabinet and took down the medicine bottle. She emptied the blue and yellow Prozac capsules into the bin and was just about to fill the bottle with the vitamin C tablets when she realised that they were completely different.

Matt realised this too. "What if she notices?" he looked worried.

"Don't be stupid," scoffed Rachel. "Mum's out of it half the time. She won't notice."

Matt could see that she was nervous too, so he looked at her sceptically until she said, "Okay. But I have an idea. Just get the Prozac tablets out of the bin and I'll tell you."

As soon as Rachel outlined the plan to Matt, he began to crush the white vitamin tablets in the heavy marble bowl that had sat forever unused on their counter top. Meanwhile Rachel began dismantling the Prozac tablets. She simply slid each end apart. They both chuckled as the contents of each capsule spilled out into the sink.

"What if they won't go back together?" Matt asked.

"Let me worry about that, Professor. You just keep grinding. And absolutely no hard bits. Here, let's try one."

Carefully, Rachel scooped some powdered vitamin C into two parts of a Prozac capsule and carefully slid them together using the tiniest swipe of homemade egg yolk glue to seal them.

"Nice and tight and totally identical, just different ingredients, expertly sealed together with my special formula," she growled in a mediocre attempt at a Transylvanian-style voice.

"Ah, I think Count Dracula just drank people's blood. He didn't mess with their tablets," Matt laughed.

"Do not mess with my tablets, Mr Dracula," Rachel continued in an even worse attempt.

"Rach, I think I want my teenage sister back. That way I know what I'm dealing with... you know, the moods, the sarcasm and the..."

"Stop it there bro! I can revert at any time. Now get a move on and keep the dust coming my way. And don't get sloppy, absolutely no lumps."

Working together, they had soon refilled almost all the Prozac capsules, with the exception of those that had gotten slightly squeezed, and put them back into their bottle.

"Why do you think this Moseley guy is hanging around Mum?" Matt asked, as Rachel finished the last capsule.

Rachel seemed to study the question before replying, "Not sure. He's way too young for her. First I sort of liked him, but now he gives me the creeps. It won't take her long before she sees through him though, I hope".

"These might just help, do you think?" Matt asked, tapping the bottle of fake Prozac.

"You bet," Rachel exclaimed, before reverting to a more Italian gangster-type voice, "and hey, put out the bin. We don't wanna leave no trace, okay bro?" They high-fived and he carried out his boss's instructions.

At ten o' clock, Ricky dropped Colette off at her house and gave her a token nod as a goodbye. When Colette walked inside, still slightly put out, she gave only a casual response to Matt and Rachel's enquiries.

"No, if you must ask, it didn't go well, thank you," she said, leaning a little too far forward. She staggered into the kitchen and dumped a bunch of flowers into the sink. Then she emerged immediately, kicked off her heels and used the bannisters to propel herself up the stairs.

Matt and Rachel exchanged puzzled glances as they watched their mother go into her room and close her door. Then they followed her up, each going to the sanctuary of their respective bedrooms.

Five minutes later, they both heard their mother calling from her bedroom.

"Sorry to bother you, Rachel love. I need a glass of water and my tablets."

"No problem, Mum," answered Rachel, "I was getting some water for myself, anyway".

"Do you think it will work?" Matt asked Mr Freckles.

The dummy stared at him with its glass eyes.

It might, but then again, it might not.

"Very supportive," Matt muttered aloud.

Hearing Rachel coming back up the stairs, Matt left his bed and tiptoed out onto the landing. Peeking over the bannisters, he was met with a 'get-back-into-your room-you-idiot' look, which he hastily obeyed.

Ah… my real sister back again, what a relief, he thought.

So be a little more civil to your loyal companion, Mr Freckles shot back.

"Thanks love," Matt heard his mother saying from the room directly across from his. "Sorry to ask, love, but there are flowers in the kitchen sink. Would you be a dear and put them into a vase for me, please. At least they were nice".

Colette's voice sounded a little slurred, as if she had had too much to drink.

As he listened to Rachel returning downstairs, Matt wondered what he might possibly do after the excitement of the evening. He wasn't in the least bit tired. It looked like his mother was going to be out of it for the night, and knowing her, that would probably go on for a few days... unless the new medicine had its desired effect. Then there was only Rachel to worry about. He didn't think she was ready for his latest revelations.

In the days since his little accident, Matt had retraced the route he had walked home from Durrow Abbey in the hope of finding his dad's letter. It seemed to have vanished on the wind, however. As he waited for Rachel to go back to bed, a madcap plan began to unfold in his brain. He decided to put it into action.

For safety sake... in case he fell down another hole somewhere, Matt decided to let his cyber friend know what he intended to do. He opened PenChat and began to type.

'Hi 101. Heading to DA. If I don't return, let someone know... please.'

- 11 -
JOURNEY INTO THE PAST

As soon as everything was quiet, Matt stuffed Mr Freckles unceremoniously into his backpack and tiptoed downstairs. In the kitchen, he grabbed his torch, the usual bags of salt and vinegar crisps, and a bottle of water and added them to the backpack. As a mad afterthought, he also included a carton of eggs. Then he opened the back door as quietly as possible, borrowed Rachel's bike and cycled off.

Stopping outside the Dinglefitz house, he stood in the shelter of the thick evergreen fence that surrounded it and prepared to hurl the eggs at one of the windows. As he tried to work out which window belonged to his tormentor's bedroom, Matt was interrupted by the sound of shouting coming from the house.

Matt hadn't meant to snoop, just a quick reconnaissance before bombardment, but it didn't take much to see that all was not well. Although he couldn't make out the voices clearly, Matt heard a man shouting at Billy in a semi-drunken voice, threatening to kill him... or something to that effect, as a woman pleaded with the man. Billy wasn't taking it lying down. He could be heard shouting back in a high-pitched, tearful voice. Matt saw the man lunge again before he disappeared from view.

Mr Freckles' voice echoed in his head. *You shouldn't meddle in these affairs, Matthew. They are not your concern. Besides, you have your own problems.*

A part of Matt was happy when he realised that his arch enemy was getting a little bit of his own medicine, but the ferocity in the man's voice frightened him. It was like nothing he had ever experienced. Leaving the eggs intact on the ground beside the fence, he got back on the bike and cycled onwards, the harsh voice of Dinglefitz's father lingering in his mind as he pedalled furiously in the direction of Durrow Abbey.

When he arrived at the Abbey, Matt walked cautiously into the cover of a spinney of yew trees before approaching the house. The old, redbrick monstrosity loomed darkly in the generous light of the moon. To a stranger, the hulking mansion would appear threatening, set as it was with the forest shrouded behind it. The unkempt borders and gardens were a sad reflection of the neglect the place had been subjected to since Matt's family left. As the full moon came out from behind a cloud, he heard a strange howl.

This is kind of like a scene from a movie, or something, thought Matt.

Be cautious, came the message, reminding him that he had Mr Freckles in tow. Advancing to the edge of the cover, he heard the rustling of leaves and light crunch of frosted grass beneath his feet.

Duck!

Matt ducked behind a bush and realised that Mr Freckles had shown perfect timing. Through gaps in the leaves and branches, he could see a man, perhaps the same man who had followed him on the first night he came.

Phew, Matt gave a sigh of relief as he watched his fellow intruder walk by. *Thank you for the warning, my wooden friend.*

He let his pursuer go on, maintaining his position but climbing the huge yew tree he had hidden behind, so as to gain a better vantage point. As he watched the skulking figure proceed along the lawn, following the line of a beech hedge, a distant memory came into Matt's mind. It was from his childhood.

He must have been about three years old, and the heat of the summer resembled a warm blanket as he played on the lawn with his parents and sister. Another memory followed the first one. This time, he was older and was searching for something in the woods nearby. In among the trees, he found an opening, a sort of hatch made out of metal, flush with the ground.

From his hiding place in the yew tree, Matt thought about that hatch. It must be here still, but it would be overgrown by now. Perhaps it might lead to something important: a tunnel perhaps, something that would bring him closer to finding some answers, tell him why he was being followed. The idea that he was being followed... hunted even... didn't sit easily with Matt.

Something crawling on Matt's leg made him jump, almost causing him to lose his grip on the tree branch. It might have been nothing more than a spider attempting to wrap him up for later, but it was enough to jolt him back to reality. This was just as well, for the man who had been skulking along the hedge earlier was now walking openly back down the avenue in Matt's direction. From his hiding place, Matt could see that the man was holding a phone and speaking in hushed tones into it.

"No, the little bugger seems to have gone to ground."

The hairs on Matt's neck stood up as he thought he recognised the voice. Had he heard it somewhere before? He just couldn't be sure. The man leaned against the trunk of the very tree where he was perched some fifteen feet above the ground. The conversation continued.

"No, not sure how much he knows. Looks like he's only fishing for clues. But if he figures anything out, you'll be the first to know. No, still no contact... yeah... yeah... I know. If I thought it would flush O'Connor out, I'd kill the lot of them, but we'd have to be sure he was around. Things are getting worse for them. The kids might even be taken from her. There'll be headlines. Then he'll make a move... yeah... will do. I know. We may have to repeat the process. No, I agree like we said, put on the pressure and he'll break cover. Don't worry boss. As soon as the kid knows anything, I'll know it."

Matt's stalker pocketed the cell phone, and taking one more glance about him, made his way back along the avenue towards the main road.

Wait, Matthew. You need to compose yourself. Let him get into his car before you move.

Matt followed Mr Freckles' advice and waited. The frost-laden air allowed the sound of the rough, heavy engine to reach him easily. Only after he was happy that it had pulled off and he was on his own did Matt descend from the cover of the branches.

After about ten minutes of continuous searching, he found a patch where more than the normal scattering of leaves had accumulated. Matt cleared them away, and there beneath them was the metal door he was looking for, flush with the earth.

"Unbelievable," Matt said, as he saw the rusted code lock. Amazingly the numbers still moved, protected as they were from the elements by a rubber flap.

"Now what am I supposed to do? Any ideas Mr Freckles?"

Think, Matthew. Think. Try the first set of numbers that come into your mind.

Matt looked at his friend, his smiling face lit by the moonlight, and keyed in the numbers 101.

The hatch unlocked and swung open, revealing some steps.

"That's too much of a coincidence, Mr F. What could possibly be down there?"

Probably a tunnel, if memory serves me correctly. By the way, did I mention that I am frightfully constrained in this rucking satchel of yours?

Matt carefully descended the steps and was halfway down before he remembered to close the hatch. When he pulled down the heavy metal door, it banged shut with a thud. Only then did Matt realise his mistake. It dawned on him that it would be impossible for him to open the hatch from his side.

Oh well, this little passage had better lead somewhere, or you are going to realise what it's like to be alone... let's hope it's a little less than last time, what?

"Thanks Mr F. Any more cheery thoughts? Or ideas maybe?"

Have you ever met Mr Harry Houdini?

"Can't say that I have. Wasn't he good at getting out of scrapes?"

Just enough illusion one might say to create dramatic interest. Now, Master Matthew, you must think of yourself as a Houdini of sorts, not in the counterfeit setting of the stage, and with no comic appendage in tow, but possessing of such an inner conviction as to render you...

"Freckles, I am afraid I might never get out of here alive, I'm up to my ankles in poo, and you are going on about the stage. If you don't want to be left in this tunnel for another seven years, please help me to get out of here."

One part of Matt was terrified, but the other was relieved and confident that he had Mr Freckles with him. If only he could stop the endless ranting! Luckily the torch lit up the curved tunnel wall, and here and there, iron-covered air holes allowed small slivers of moonlight to enter.

Matt contemplated trying to climb up to one of these vents, but the heavy bars that covered them appeared capable of withstanding more than his feeble strength. The walls were damp to the touch, and stalactites hung like protective spears in places from the ceiling. Eventually, Matt came to a heavy iron door. The door handle turned easily, and Matt pushed hard, but although the door seemed to give a little at the top, it appeared to be stuck fast at the bottom.

"What now?"

Now we wait.

"What?"

I just wanted to say that. A sense of humour is a wonderful thing you know, especially in a situation of crisis.

Matt waited. There wasn't much else he could do.

With the passage of time, the door has become fused in places, due in no small part, I suspect to the accumulation of damp and rust. But if rust is formed from moisture, then it can be relieved from moisture.

"What do you mean?"

My use of the word, 'relieved' is quite deliberate and should give you a clue as to a possible solution.

"Sorry?"

Not being human, a condition I seldom crave I assure you, I lack the necessary equipment to produce the moisture to... ahem... relieve the situation. Uric acid should do the trick if...

"Euww! Okay, I get it. You want me to... right. Better idea, I'll just get my bottle of water and pour it on," Matt said throwing off the backpack and rummaging down beside Mr Freckles.

Stop. That tickles. I had more than enough of that from your ancestor, and by the way, you need to listen to me now. A word of caution; as you might be some time in these caverns you should drink the water and then do as I instructed. An indelicacy, I admit, but a necessary one, both for your own survival and my constitution.

Reluctantly, Matt did as Mr Freckles had suggested. When he tried the door again, it gave way, and Matt walked through it into what he quickly ascertained was the basement of Durrow Abbey. The room was filled with every sort of dusty junk; old toys, furniture that looked like it belonged in a museum, old paintings, a wooden rocking horse and many household appliances. He swung his torch around, and a set of sharp white teeth was suddenly caught in its beam. The teeth were surrounded by wide, red jaws that were displayed in all their frightening glory. Matt screamed and dropped the torch. For a few seconds pitch blackness reigned supreme once again. Matt dropped to his knees and began to grope around.

Left a little… forward now… there.

"Thanks. Wow, what is that thing?"

Matt finally found his torch, and shining it upwards, realised that what he had seen was a gigantic stuffed brown bear.

Ah, I didn't tell you about the time Charles and I went to India, did I? Quite the sportsman, was your great…

"It's fine, really. I just want to know which door to take."

There are only two, and you've just come in through one of them.

The door out of the basement opened easily, and the small number of steps on the other side brought Matt up into a large, windowless room. The room seemed comfortable and was equipped with many of the comforts of a modern apartment, as if someone had spent a considerable amount of time there.

Matt's torch found an extension cord, which he followed to a switch on the wall. Without holding out too much hope, he flicked the switch. Amazingly, two lamps came on. Matt was standing in front of a mirror and his reflection, complete with that of Mr Freckles looking garishly out over his shoulder, made him jump with fright for the third time that night.

The floor was covered in bright wood, very different from the dark flagstones that covered much of his childhood home, but it gave the place a homely feel. Over the mirror was a crest with its sword-wielding knight, emblazoned with the O'Connor family motto: *Ó Dhia gach aon chabhair.*

Opposite Matt was a table and beyond that, a bed, raised off the floor by a series of large books, many of which had the same O'Connor crest on their spines. The bedclothes were fresh and were covered by an expensive looking green-checked blanket. In one corner, there was a spiral iron staircase, leading to a hole in the ceiling. There was no fridge or kitchen, but an old sideboard held glasses and various bottles of drinks. Among these, Matt found something that rang a bell with him; a trophy-shaped bottle of the most expensive looking perfume he had ever seen. Around its neck was a silver tassel that was gathered in by a gold seal. The bottle read, *Shalimar* and underneath was inscribed, "Perfume Initial". Matt couldn't resist a sniff. The rich, spicy aroma brought him back to his childhood, to excursions into his mother's bedroom, to times when she had snuggled him close. It was her smell, and only one person could have put it there. He decided to take it with him and, disregarding the protests of his passenger, plonked it into his backpack. On a nearby desk, Matt noticed a folder, a sort of scrapbook. Sitting in a chair beside the desk, he opened the scrapbook and began to read the newspaper cuttings that were glued to its pages.

DISAPPEARANCE OF FAMOUS JEWELS

The O'Connor family, Ronan, Colette, Rachel (8) and Matt (5) are the rightful keepers of the famous Irish Crown Jewels, which vanished last night, the 13th of February, 2007. It is believed that a gang of three arrived in a white transit van, broke into the O'Connor house, and attempted a tiger-style raid in which Mrs O'Connor and her children were taken prisoner. The purpose of this action was, in the opinion of the police, to pressurise Mr O'Connor into handing over this priceless piece of Irish history, namely, the Irish Crown Jewels. This raid was not successful, as Colette and her two children were concealed in a hidden room while Ronan O'Connor, it is speculated, made off through the woods with the jewels. The frustrated thieves set fire to the stable yard and destroyed the recently restored church. Mrs O'Connor and her two children were found shortly afterwards in an abandoned vehicle and were taken to hospital where they were treated for smoke inhalation and shock. Police are requesting anyone with information regarding the thieves or any sightings of Ronan O'Connor, who has not yet returned to his family, to come forward immediately. When questioned by this reporter, Colette O'Connor said that her husband, Ronan, was more important to her than any jewels, and that any information, however little it may be, would be greatly appreciated.
Camilla McLoughlin

And then from another paper, *The Tullamore Tribune*, from Friday of the same week.

LOCAL FAMILY TARGETED

A tiger-style raid, which targeted the O'Connor residence in Durrow, Tullamore, County Offaly, has left the local community in shock. When flames from the stable area were spotted by nearby residents, they called the Guards and the fire department. Arriving quickly on the scene, members of the emergency services found a portion of the house and the extensive stables on fire. Police also heard from a witness, a nanny, who reported that a man, believed to be Ronan O'Connor, slipped into the forest with a large black box. There are also reports of shots being fired at the scene, and Mr O'Connor, or some of the raiders, may have been wounded in the altercation. Police have cordoned off the area and are conducting a search of the vast wooded area that surrounds Durrow Abbey. The public is alerted to be on the lookout for any suspicious activity, and police have appealed for information on the whereabouts of Mr O'Connor. If anyone has any information they should call the local Gardaí on 0506-32000. Ronan O'Connor has not been seen since the incident, and there are fears for his safety. The other family members, Mrs Colette O'Connor and her two young children, were found tied and gagged in an abandoned Ford Transit van. They were immediately taken to Tullamore General Hospital and were held under the protection of an armed Garda unit before being treated and released into the care of relatives. Although not harmed, they are traumatised by the episode and are said to be in considerable shock. The house was partially damaged by the fire and the family will have to be cared for by relatives for the foreseeable future.

Ger Scully

Once Matt finished reading the article, a vision from his past came into his head. He was no longer sitting on the comfortable swivel chair. He was five years old and was in his bedroom in Durrow Abbey. Shouts could be heard from the corridor outside his bedroom, and Matt started to cry. He opened his door and saw smoke at one end of the hall. He ran in the opposite direction and opened the hidden door at the end of the passageway. Outside in the cold, night air, he could see his dad running away. Colette came running over and picked him up, but the criminals found them and tied them up in a van. All of them were screaming for help.

"Mum! Rachel!" Matt screamed, but his vision had ended. Shaking, Matt went over and lay down on the comfortable bed. He felt safe here, comforted. He removed the perfume bottle and took another sniff, relaxing in the comfort and the vague but happy memory it brought him. He realised that he shouldn't relax too much or he might fall asleep, but he couldn't stop himself. He let it happen, glad to slip into the world of dreams.

But this dream, when it came, was like nothing Matt had ever experienced before. He felt as if he was hovering above himself. He was dreaming that he was watching himself have a dream. *Weird,* he thought.

Matt was moving, but not of his own accord. It seemed as if there was a magnet pulling him towards a massive fridge. He was moving through the air towards the wall! He was going to crash!

"Aaah" Matt breathed, relieved and partly shocked. When he had reached the wall, he had just passed harmlessly through, which was simultaneously cool and terrifying. He hovered in mid-air just outside Durrow Abbey.

It was as if Matt were watching a movie with his finger pressed down on the fast forward button. The images around him sped up. He was in the stable yard, and all around him there was fire. He could see figures through the thick, black smog and could just make out three people on the ground below. One of them Matt knew immediately.

"Mum," he whispered, "so they must be... " He looked at the other two, one of whom was a young blonde girl, Rachel. The smallest of the three was a tiny black-haired boy with bright, terrified eyes. In a heartbeat, Matt knew that he was looking at his younger self. Out of the corner of his eye he saw movement. He saw his father, holding a huge black case, running into the woods. He could see his father's face.

"No!" Matt screamed, "Dad, come back! Dad!" His father turned, but instead of helping his son, he stared straight through him.

"Oh... Dear God, no," Matt whimpered. Now, he could see the

black-suited men dragging his younger self away, along with Colette and Rachel, all of them screaming at the top of their lungs.

Matt thought he would be sick, but a voice surprised him.

Hello Matt. He twisted around and saw Mr Freckles standing in front of him, on nothing but air, smiling as if they were doing something as ordinary as meeting for lunch.

Matt felt dizzy, and just when he thought things couldn't get worse, he started to drift off again, faster and faster. He could hear Mr Freckles shouting something, but the words were lost to the wind. Then, he was back in the comfortable bed. The vision was over, and he was sitting bolt upright in a cold sweat.

"What... on... Earth." Matt knew his dream had meant something, but what?

He pulled Mr Freckles out of his backpack.

"I had the weirdest dream."

I know, I gave it to you.

"You did? How, and why?"

You needed to know what happened, for all of our sakes.

"But I still don't know where my dad went."

You'll find out eventually, when the time is right.

"But why did he leave?"

It was his duty, his family duty. He had to protect the jewels. He told you that in his letter.

"The stables were burning," remembered Matt, "and... and... people, criminals with guns went around searching for something".

Yes, money and riches are a terrible temptation.

"But why did you show me the dream now?"

The time is right.

"What on Earth is that supposed to mean?" Matt said, getting frustrated.

Please, I am weary now. I require rest.

"What? You're fine. Please tell me what it means," Matt begged.

Mr Freckles seemed to sigh almost visibly before his voice appeared in Matt's head once again.

You are the lucky one. Lucky, you slept through the first stage of the raid, the break-in. You were woken up by your mother, in mindless panic, taking you and Rachel to the tunnels that were made for safety and escape. Your mother was afraid. She had begged your father to come to safety, but he told her to go without him.

Matt leaned against the wall, putting a pillow behind his head, getting ready for the most important story of his life.

Your father told your mother that he had to protect the jewels. He locked the trap door saying, 'I love you,' before fleeing out of a window. He hopped off the roof to see that the place that was your home was a partially burning wreck, and the stables were a total inferno. He ran away with a big black case in his hand. Later on, shots were exchanged. A man died, and your mother didn't know whether your father was alive or dead. You insisted on coming back for me, your loyal friend, but you dropped me in the tunnel. That was the last I would see of you, or any other human soul, for that matter, for seven long years. When you and your mother and sister emerged from the fox hole, you were captured by the gang, but only for a short while it seems. For some reason or another, you were abandoned by the raiders. This part, I am unable to comment on as I wasn't present, having had to make my way back through the tunnel before finding sanctuary in the secret compartment where I waited... and waited. Without human interaction, my powers lessened more and more, and increasingly so with the passage of further time. Movement is the first to go. It was all I could do over the long, dark years to fend off the scurrying mice that came about me in the empty darkness of that grotesque place. But enough about me, Master Matthew. It is high time you made your journey homeward, is it not?

Groggily, Matt rose, reluctant to leave the familiar comfort of the enclosed room. He unplugged the power cables from their sockets and by the light of his torch, climbed the spiral staircase, which led into the main hall. He found the bars that he had escaped through on his first visit and squeezed through them again.

Matt was amazed to see that an orange haze was beginning to creep over the trees to the east. Soft blankets of fog were beginning to make way for the day ahead. No sooner had Matt crunched the frosty gravel to the front of the house than the alarmed crowing of a disturbed cock pheasant alerted the woodland to the presence of an intruder. The alarm was magnified by a pair of cackling magpies who, it seemed, were anxious to escort him off the property. The calls brought to mind a long forgotten memory he had of standing behind a man with a shotgun. They were at the edge of this very same wood, watching pigeons cannon up into the heights before swooping at speed, then gliding to their night roosts in the tallest branches.

He wanted to remember more, but the knowledge that he had been away from his home for nearly the entire night, just days after going missing and ending up in hospital, spurred him to get on Rachel's bicycle and cycle quickly home.

It was six in the morning when Matt sneaked back into his house. Luckily, all was quiet.

- 12 -

MR FRECKLES VS PEECEE

M r Freckles eased himself out of his corner, using his short, stiff limbs independently for the first time in many, many years.

With young Matthew away at school, this is a perfect opportunity to master this instrument.

He heaved himself up onto the desk chair. It immediately swivelled around and he fell off.

Confounded contraption. Why would anyone bother to invent such a stupid chair?

Mr Freckles got jerkily to his feet and eyed the chair warily. He had to attempt it three more times before he was able to climb up and stay on. The next confusing thing was finding the "on" button for the communicating machine. He thought back to all the times that he had seen Matt turn it on. His roving eyes landed on a small round button. He lifted his creaking left arm and jabbed a finger at it. *The confounded thing... it is on at last, but...* Mr Freckles stared at his left hand, which had come unattached and was lying on the carpet. *I am going to need that*, he thought.

He focused with all his might until the arm began to twitch and then slowly drag itself in his direction before shooting into its socket.

Better. One must be in possession of all of one's limbs and faculties if one is to conquer this dratted Peecee. He began to stare in the direction of the computer screen. This was not just a staring contest; this was a battle of wills. Neither man would look away.

I will get the better of you, you wretched contraption! Mr Freckles frowned. He had just realised that Peecee had no eyes.

Err... You may have won this battle, but I will win the war!

I must get into the computer's brain. He scanned the keyboard before settling on the "enter" key as he focused all his hypnotic energy on entering the inner thoughts of the machine.

All these damned wires... red, blue, black, oh! What's this? PenChat. This must be how it speaks. I've got you now! Hmmm... I should go carefully, making sure I do not damage the contraption. I just need to get rid of that Moseley, or I could... destroy the entire machine. But better to destroy a machine than a family.

Mr Freckles was on a roll. He cursed the different coloured wires and pressed the delete button repeatedly.

Perfect. He looked at the screen to admire his handy work.

Arrghh! A pop-up advertisement had suddenly appeared on the screen, and the picture that featured on it caused Mr Freckles to wish that he could close his eyes.

You, you stupid mechanical thingy-a-magigy! He summoned up the most insulting name he could think of. *You think I will be frightened away by such tactics! I will beat you.*

He hem, Mr Freckles gave a little cough and addressed the woman on the screen. *You have two choices; after you cover yourself up, that is; you may leave this screen straight away and I will not report you to the relevant authorities, or I will make you leave.*

The woman on the screen stayed obstinately silent. *You have chosen the hard way.* Mr Freckles' wooden finger hovered over the delete button. *Any last words? Well then, goodbye.* Mr Freckles pressed the delete button yet again.

Nothing happened. He pressed it again. Still, nothing happened.

Arrgh! Mr Freckles slammed his hands on the keyboard in frustration. The woman disappeared. *Yes!"* But in her place came a never-ending cycle of pop-up ads.... *NO!! You, you, I can't even come up with a foul enough name to describe you, if only I could get rid of these intrusive thingies. I don't want 50 percent off bikini waxing or a voucher for a salon.*

Mr Freckles slumped against the computer, defeated. His head accidently hit the off button. He glanced at the PC, hearing the beep from the button. The screen was blank. *Yes! I have conquered you. Never again will you mock me. Goodbye you commercial announcements. Goodbye you half-naked harlot. I have won!*

***

Matt dragged himself up the stairs, exhausted from the exertions of the previous night and dwelling on what an awful day it had been. The only good thing was that David had promised to visit later that evening and the intriguing memories of Matt's most recent trip to Durrow Abbey. Those same memories had got him into trouble for daydreaming in three classes.

Thinking about the extraordinary events had done him little good, because he didn't know who to turn to with his newly acquired information. He couldn't just plonk the perfume in front of his mother with the entire story. She didn't let him in on her feelings, and since their recent conversation, she had made it very clear that any mention of their past life was off limits. He wondered why his mother had brought them back to Tullamore. She was supposed to have an open door into her old job at the hospital, but her depression meant that this was unlikely to happen. Surely it was only a matter of time before the hospital got tired of her messing them about.

The day had been a mind-boggling jumble of confusing thoughts. If only he could make contact with his dad, thought Matt, his problems might be solved. He decided that he would have to call into Agatha again to see if she had been able to make contact. Before leaving for school, he had boldly left the scrapbook he had found in Durrow Abbey in Rachel's top drawer. His hope was that she would find it and finally talk to him about the past.

Matt heard Mr Freckles speaking before he opened the bedroom door.

Is there something wrong, Master Matthew?

"Oh nothing."

Matt walked into his room and sat on his bed, not taking his eyes off the ground.

You're welcome.

"For what?"

Caring for your peecee, while you were away.

139

"WHAT?" Matt looked up quickly.

Your Peecee, Mr Freckles explained patiently. *It became very ill while you were at school, a virus, it would seem.*

Matt looked past Mr Freckles and saw a sticky substance on the keyboard and white powder smothering his mouse.

"How did it get a virus?"

I don't know. I'm a ventriloquist's dummy not a vet. But whatever I did put it to sleep, so don't go poking at it.

Matt walked over to his desk and sat down.

"OWWWWW!" He sat back up again. His swivel chair had been covered in needles! "What's this about?" he shrieked.

Shhhh, you'll wake it. If you must know, I found them in your first aid kit. I think they are called Epeee Pens, which is queer considering they are not pens at all.

Matt massaged his sore backside and groaned, "Why did you do this...?"

Well, you see, your minion AVG popped up and said your pet Peecee had a virus, and I immediately sprang into action. I have a vast range of knowledge on this sort of thing you know. It felt very hot, so I put a wet cloth on its forehead, I'm not sure that I got it in the right spot though.

Matt noticed a dripping wet sock resting on his monitor.

"Noooo," he wailed. He carefully removed the syringes and his duvet, which had been draped over the keyboard and the lower part of the screen.

A quick reboot and ctrl-Z restored everything in a matter of seconds.

Oh blast, I thought it was better to give the poor wee thing a bit of a rest.

"Freckles, I want you to stay away from my computer. Am I making myself clear?"

Perfectly.

- 13 -

SUSPICIONS

M att heard a car pull up in the driveway.
"Yes!" he exclaimed, "David's here!"

He ran downstairs and opened the front door.

"Hi David! Rachel's gone out with Sandy, so we have the house to ourselves."

"Cool, but where is your mum?"

"Oh yeah... well, she's asleep."

David's eyes registered surprise. "She must be really tired. My dad works shifts too. When you come over to my house, we'll have to be really quiet until about seven. Don't worry, I know the drill."

The two boys made their way into the kitchen.

"Are you hungry?" asked Matt.

"Nah, I'm fine. You wanna play monopoly? I have it in my bag."

"Yeah, let's play!"

After a few enjoyable hours of monopoly, Matt and David retreated into Matt's room with a couple of bags of crisps. They sat on his bed happily munching Taytos.

"Where is that dummy you had the last time I was here?" asked David, with a hint of a smile.

Matt chuckled. "I put him under my bed. I didn't want to scare you again."

"Good, I must have jumped a foot in the air!"

They both collapsed on the bed laughing.

"So," said Matt, trying to get over the giggles, "do you want to play computer games?"

"Sure. You have WOW open. Is it online?"

"Yes. Just give me two seconds."

"I play this all the time, but my dad insists on looking at the chat box when I'm finished."

"That's an invasion of your privacy, isn't it? Does he really check it?"

"Occasionally. I don't mind though. Once we get past all the stupid questions he asks, over and over again, why should I care?"

"Wow level 79, I can only get to level 65!" said Matt admiringly as they played.

"I can teach you the special trick to move you up," David offered confidently.

"Cool." But wait, look, a message from Noname." He logged on to PenChat and read the message.

'Hi 102, I'm really bored. Wanna chat?'

'Sorry 101,' Matt typed, 'I can't talk now. Maybe later?"

Just as Matt was about to press send, David interrupted.

"No, it's okay. I'd like to speak with this ehh... person with you."

"Are you sure?"

"Yeah."

Matt erased the previous message and wrote 'Yeah, 101, that would be cool. My friend David is here too!'

"Matt," said David, "I don't want my name written on the Internet. Do you mind erasing it?"

"No problem!" replied Matt as he typed. "Fixed."

They soon heard a beep that was Noname's reply: 'So Matt, I was thinking we could use Whatsapp to talk more freely.'

Matt looked puzzled.

'How do you know my name?' he typed.

After a long pause, Noname101 replied, 'Oh you must have mentioned it sometime. Anyway, did you hear from your dad?'

Matt was about to reply, but David stopped him, "Matt! He knows your name!"

"So, he's a friend!"

"You don't know that... for sure."

"Yes I do," replied Matt huffily. "Anyways it's no big deal. I must have told him by accident."

"It's none of my business, Matt but it's a little weird to be talking to this guy. How much do you really know about him?"

"Not a lot."

"But he knows a lot about you. Like where you go to school, where you live, where you used to live, your family. You've told him everything."

A little taken aback, Matt was unsure what to say.

David continued, "Do you mind if I ask him a few questions, just to see what he says?"

"No, sure. Be my guest."

David began to type. "Where's this guy from?" he asked Matt as his nimble fingers flew across the keyboard.

"Athlone, I think," Matt replied, "and you'd better slow down a little or he'll know it's not me."

He still wasn't comfortable with David's idea, but by now, a long sentence had been written. David showed it to him before sending it.

'You know I don't like talking about the past,' went the message. 'The future is more exciting. It must be great to live in Athlone. Does your dad live with you?'

There was no answer.

David sent a second message.

'I don't mean to pry. It's just that you know so much about me and... I'd like to get to know you better...'

Again, no message came back.

David continued. 'My friends have the app you mentioned, but I don't have a phone. Remember I told you?'

'What friends?' This time, the reply was immediate.

"I don't like this guy," David said. "He doesn't seem to want to answer questions, he just asks them."

"But he's been nice to me... when I had no one to talk to. I know all about his school, his favourite games, movies, loads of stuff."

"Okay, so do you want me to stop?" David said apologetically. "Did he ever ask to meet you?"

"Now you're giving me the creeps."

"Can I just try one more thing, and you can stop me if you're not happy with it?"

David typed slowly and thoughtfully this time.

'Friends, yeah, you're right. Don't have too many. Would you like to meet up sometime? In Athlone, where you live? I could go up on the bus. You could show me around. Whatcha think?'

"What if he says yes?" Matt asked.

"I don't know. Maybe we go and get there before him. See what he's like. If we're not happy, we just scarper. It might be fun."

"Yeah, fun. Rachel would kill me."

"Only if she found out."

They had barely sent the message when the reply flashed on screen,

'When?'

They looked at each other in amazement. David started typing again.

'Not sure. Just a crazy idea. I'd have to do a bunk from school. Maybe next week. Or the week after.

'Maybe.'

'See ya.'

David closed the dialogue box then jumped up from the chair and dived onto Matt's bed.

"That's crazy, Matt. I shouldn't have done that."

"Yeah crazy," Matt agreed, "and stupid."

"Sorry, Matt."

"It might be fun though."

"How would we get there?"

"Kearns' bus. It leaves every hour from Main Street."

"I don't have much money," Matt said.

"Not a problem. It's only eight euro for under sixteens. I have a stash."

"Wow!"

"Yeah, I'm mega wealthy. Savings you know. Must have all of 28, maybe 30, euros squirreled away."

They both laughed.

"Come on, let's play another game," Matt suggested.

A few hours later, the two boys were watching TV in the sitting room when they heard a car horn from outside.

"That's my mum," said David, "Bye!"

"See you in school tomorrow," replied Matt.

"Okay. And it's a secret right?"

"Yeah, secret."

- 14 -

AN UNEXPECTED MEETING

Colette walked towards the school with a new spring in her step. It was more than a week since Matt and Rachel had switched her pills, and she was feeling a whole lot better. She walked into the foyer and was approached by a man in a navy suit and royal blue tie.

"How are you? Ah, Mrs O'Connor, I presume?"

"Yes, and ah, very well, thank you."

Colette walked into the school and surveyed the surroundings.

"This is a really lovely school you've got here Mr Watson."

"It's your first time here, I think? And please call me Joseph. You must have trusted your children to make their own way in when they started."

"I was happy with everything. The children showed me the website, and I once spoke to your secretary. She seemed nice."

"Indeed."

Mr Watson escorted Colette into his office, which was near the back of the school. There were two glass sliding doors built into an orangey-red wall. On the far wall was an enormous window that looked out over a large field. The principal gestured towards a seat in front of his spotless desk. Colette sat, taking in the contents of the room. On her right, there was a bookcase made of dark wood. The wall opposite was lined with filing cabinets. Mr Watson sat down in front of her.

"Well," he began, "Rachel is doing well. She has fitted in, from what her year head tells me. My main concern is Matt. He is being bullied, and there have been incidents, as you probably know. He has also scored very low in most of his tests, slipping from his Naas results."

"Oh," said Colette "Ah, I will try to help him to bring those grades back up to scratch."

"Well, I believe depression could be the cause of it. If so, it's going to take a lot more work to bring up his grades."

"A child can't be depressed, can they?"

"Indeed they can, just not in exactly the same way as adults. For children, it involves being constantly unhappy and not caring about school and..."

"Oh, I wasn't aware."

"Yes, that is the problem, not many people are. Anyway, as you know, he has been seeing the school counsellor."

"Well... "

"You should know that! I left you several messages, but you did not get back to me."

"He mentioned it... once, or twice maybe."

"Yes. I believe he is missing a strong role model in his life. I believe it may be part of the reason why he is finding it difficult to assert himself", Mr Watson speculated.

"Well it's your job to help him, is it not?"

"Yes," said Mr Watson patiently, "but it's not only my job, or the school's. We need support, especially from parents."

Colette began to feel frustrated. "Uhh... well."

"The counsellor asked him to make a list of things that trouble him," the principal added, "and Matt agreed to share them with us and you."

"And?"

The principal took out a sheet of paper.

"This is Matt's list of things that trouble him: 'my family, safety, Pimple Face (Billy Dinglefitz) and Ricky Moseley. Do you know anything about this?"

"Yes, some of it." Colette was stunned. "I'll do my best to try and sort this out."

"And another thing, Mrs O'Connor, a social service worker named John Flanagan sent me a letter. I am duty-bound to discuss it with you".

He pulled open a drawer under his desk and removed a white envelope. He opened it and read it aloud:

Dear Principal,

Following communication with the Gardaí, it has been brought to my attention that Mrs Colette O'Connor, a parent of children attending your school, may be experiencing some difficulties in her role as caregiver to the minors Matt and Rachel O'Connor.

We have some concerns in relation to the matter and we wish to make an appointment to discuss some of these concerns with you as school principal. I would appreciate if you would contact our office on the above number to arrange this meeting.

Yours faithfully,

John Flanagan.

"Oh," said Colette. "This all happened before, when I was having difficulty coping with everything in my life. I have turned things around now. "

"Good," said Mr Watson "I'm delighted to hear you're better".

"Yes," said Colette. "I actually have my old job back. It's going very well."

"I'll send the good news to John Flanagan as soon as possible, that you're up and about and working. Now, we'll leave it there for today then, unless you have any questions for me?"

"Er... yes. I mean no," Colette was confused.

"Well, for our part, we'll keep an eye on Billy Dinglefitz, the one who has been bothering your Matt. If you call back in a week or two, we can review the situation. Meanwhile, I'll let you enjoy the Autumn sun while it lasts." The principal showed Colette to the door, with a pleasant smile.

***

Bounding down the stairs early that evening, Matt was assaulted by the aroma of cooking. Something significant was roasting in the oven. As he landed on the bottom step, he noticed that his mother, wearing an apron, was busy at some kind of creamy creation. He stopped and stared.

Colette smiled at him. "No need to rub it in, Mattie. This is me, and I am making a marvellous dessert to follow our scintillating, roast and stuffed chicken dinner. Where are you off to?"

"Ah, I'm just out for a minute. Be right back."

"All right, but no more than twenty minutes now, mind."

Wow, thought Matt as he pedalled away. Not a bad day after all. And it's just about to get better.

***

Rachel walked to the corner shop on Barrack Street and stood by the display window, where a variety of notices advertised lost pets, cleaning services, second-hand cars and other items for sale. Opening her bag, she fished out a piece of paper and a roll of Sellotape. As she did this, something told her that she was being watched. Rachel froze for a couple of seconds and then whipped around.

Bang.

Rachel groaned. She had hit her head off a tall steel post that ran alongside the door of the shop.

"Are you okay?"

Rachel turned to face the man who had spoken. He was tall and had brown hair. Rachel's hand reached up to her head and felt what was rapidly becoming a medium-sized lump.

"Yeah, I'm grand," she lied.

"So, you're a babysitter?"

Feeling uncomfortable, Rachel glanced down at the poster in her hand.

"Yep," She placed it on the window and stuck it up with Sellotape.

"You know," he began, "I have two children at home. A four-year-old and a two-year-old, and I have to go out tonight. Would you mind if I hired you?"

"I... yeah... sure!" Rachel hoped that she did not look as stunned as she felt. Her head told her that it was wrong to trust this stranger off the street, no matter how friendly he seemed. He was strangely familiar, though, and she felt comfortable in his presence.

"Could you manage seven or half past at the latest?"

"Yeah," said Rachel, "seven is perfect!"

"I live at number twelve, Green Meadows. Do you know where that is?"

"Sure, it's near my estate."

"Will your mother be alright with that?" the man asked, watching intently for Rachel's response. "Ask her when you get home. Here's my number so you can contact me if something crops up."

He wrote down the number on a piece of paper and handed it to her.

"Oh, my mum won't mind."

"Are you sure? Well ask her anyway just in case."

"See you later then," said Rachel.

When she got home, she asked Matt what he thought.

"Should I do it?"

"Yeah, go for it," he replied. "It's a way to get your hands on some money?"

"Yeah, I suppose."

At a quarter to seven, Rachel left the house and headed for Green Meadows. She knocked on the door and then took a step back. A few seconds later, the man opened it.

"Hello again," he said.

"Hi," said Rachel.

He led Rachel down a bare corridor. At the end of it they turned to the right into what looked like a sitting room. It had a plasma screen television in one corner, and a sofa and two armchairs lined up against the walls. The television was showing some soap or other, and Rachel could hear a couple squabbling in it. The man asked Rachel to sit down. She did so and looked around. The room was very bare. There were no signs of anything to do with children.

"Where are the kids?"

"About that," he said "I don't have any kids, well, not the ones I made up. I have two alright, and I think you already know them."

It took a moment for Rachel to take this in. "Say what?"

"Rachel, this is going to come as a shock to you but... " the man took a deep breath and released it. "Rachel, my real name is Ronan. I'm your father."

Rachel stood up, shocked. *He wasn't*, she thought. *He couldn't be.*

He opened his arms awkwardly, as if for a hug. She hit him in the chest so hard that her hand hurt.

"You're not my dad, you weirdo!" shouted Rachel. "My dad's gone! He left us and no matter what my brother says, he's never coming back, and now someone I don't even know is making fun of the fact that I'll never ever see him again."

Rachel felt tears running down her cheeks, which made her even more angry. How dare this stranger lie to just make fun of her? She'd never even met him before!

"I'm telling the truth Ra..."

"No, you're not! You can't be! Liar! Let me out of here!"

"Rachel, please... "

"Shut up. Shut up. Shut up. I don't want to hear any more lies," she screamed and tried to run past the man, but he was blocking her path.

"Rachel," the man put his hands on her shoulders. "Just listen, please. If I wasn't your father, how would I know about the time you fell over my bike and smacked your head on the concrete when you were just learning to walk? Colette and I drove you to A&E, and you sat on her lap. You ended up getting six stitches in your forehead. How would I know that?"

"How do I know? You could have asked him, couldn't you?"

"Rachel, please. I'm sorry I left, I really am."

"If you are my dad, why did you leave?"

"Rachel, I can't tell you just yet. It's too dangerous."

Rachel found herself believing him, understanding now why he had looked so familiar, but this just made her even more angry. She pushed him away and pummelled him with her fists, an uncontrollable rage taking over.

"You left us all alone, with no home, no money, no nothing! How could you abandon us like that?"

"I'm... "

"Sorry doesn't cut it! For a massive chunk of our lives, we had to fend for ourselves! Mum's been bedridden with depression, so I had to do everything, all because of you! I hate you!"

Sobbing, Rachel fell onto a chair. Ronan pulled her back up gently and hugged her.

"I missed you Rachel, more than I will ever be able to tell you."

Ever so slowly, Rachel allowed herself to be taken into her father's arms, surrendering herself finally to his embrace. "I missed you too," she murmured softly as she felt the welcome security of his warm and loving arms.

Ronan looked at her seriously.

"Now Rachel, I haven't been a father to you, and I can't be for a while longer. No family should have to endure what I have put mine through. But I am going to have to ask another sacrifice of you, and that is your silence. I don't want you to tell anyone about me. Not your mother, not even Matt. Not yet."

"Why?"

"I'll tell you soon. But Rachel, my love, you'll have to promise not to tell a soul, no matter how much you want to. Will you promise to keep my secret, just for a little while longer?"

"I promise."

- 15 -

ATHLONE

Matt woke up with a start after an unsettled night's sleep. The misgivings he had been having about skiving off school and snooping on someone who had been his friend had played on his mind, even while he slept. Ordinarily, he would sleep through any kind of noise, but this time, he had been disturbed by every gentle tap the branches of the nearby tree made against his window. He was worried. What if he got into trouble in school? The hassle of that would be the last thing his mother needed, just when she was getting well again.

As the moon broke from behind the clouds and flooded Matt's room with blue-tinged light, Mr Freckles' eyes flashed open. His perch on the laundry basket was suddenly caught in the spotlight of the slanted beam of light. *I never could resist the limelight*, he quipped cheekily.

Matt tried to ignore his wooden friend, but Mr Freckles was wide awake now. *Don't try to fool the master, young Matthew. Did you know that the Earl of Bridgewater used to dine with a dozen dogs? A wealthy patron of the arts in whose house your great great grandfather Charles and I had the pleasure of dining...*

"But you can't eat!" Matt groaned.

Ha, I knew it. You are wide awake, just like your old chum. The Earl was the one who lived out the old adage; "a man's best friend is his dog." Did you know that?

Matt ignored this senseless piece of information, but Mr Freckles continued. He was in a frivolous mood.

It may have been 1827 or maybe '28, when Charles and I were guests of his in Paris...

"Please," Matt implored, "I am trying to sleep".

No, you're not. You're worried aren't you?

Matt didn't respond.

You are fretting that you will ferret out a lie. And a liar. You're worried that someone you believed in is a fraud, a scoundrel.

"I'm worried that you will make me wake my mother. Can you please be quiet and let me get back to sleep?"

Matt was cross now, and his tone seemed to have the desired effect. Mr Freckles' wooden jaw clamped shut with a resounding snap. Matt did his usual trick of lying absolutely still and counting his own breaths until he began to lose track of the numbers. Just as he began to drift off, a new message filtered into his thoughts.

You take care, young Matthew.

"I will," he whispered back before drifting off to sleep.

The morning came too quickly. Matt's solid slumber was broken by the force of someone shaking his shoulder. It was Rachel, fully dressed in her school uniform.

"You'll have me late too, if you don't get your lazy carcass out of that bed."

"Wha... what time is it?" Matt asked, partly to his sister and partly to the disappearing bedclothes, as they flew off his bed.

"Time to move it," she sniped. "You might be able to wake up like a normal person if you weren't talking to your freaky friend."

Rachel left the room and thundered down the stairs.

Matt's concerns about the upcoming deception were now multiplied by ten. *What if we get into serious trouble?* he thought. *What if Noname turns out to be someone else?* These and other worries raced around his mind as he threw his essentials into his backpack: torch, money, change of clothes, a map of Athlone he had printed off the Internet and his school diary, with the forged note from his mother.

David was standing at the school gate, trying to appear cool, when Matt arrived.

"You still up for this?" Matt asked him.

"Inspector Clouseau, at your service." David laughed confidently. "I've been thinking," he added, "the notes are a bad idea. It's better if we just leave once we are seen at assembly".

"Okay."

The boys made their way to the assembly hall, making sure to talk to the school secretary, the principal and anyone else who wasn't teaching them that day. They stood beside one of the side doors, and just before the morning prayer was due to begin, they slipped out of the building, dodging past a few stragglers.

At the gymnasium locker rooms, the two boys changed into jeans, runners and hoodies, making themselves look just like any normal pair of twelve-year-olds. Then, they left the school and ran across Market Square. Even though it was twenty past nine in the morning, a group of idle youths had assembled close to some public benches and were right in their way. With their dark, baggy clothes that sent out a "don't-come-anywhere-near-me" message, they looked as if they might pose a problem to the truants.

Both boys sensed the danger at the same time.

David said under his breath, "Don't look in their direction, don't speed up, just keep your eyes facing forward."

"Hey, look what we have here," came a taunting voice.

From the corner of his eye, Matt made out a bare-armed figure turning in their direction.

"Two little girls on a day off from school! Do your mammies know ye're on the mitch?"

Ignoring the catcalls, David kept a steady pace, skirting round the group. Resisting the urge to look, Matt tried to stay calm, although the hairs were standing up on his neck.

By the time the two boys reached the bus stop, Kearns' bus had just closed its doors and was waiting at the traffic lights. Matt and David ran across the street and stood at the bus door, gesturing imploringly at the driver.

The doors opened with an ear-splitting hiss, almost hitting David in the face. Soon they were scrambling for two seats together, the forward motion of the bus propelling them towards the back. The only two seats available were mid-way back, one on each side of the aisle. David took the one beside a middle-aged lady with shopping bags and Matt sat beside a red-faced elderly gentleman, who greeted him immediately.

"I didn't know the schools were out, or are you young fellas on a bit of an excursion?"

The old man smelled of stale cigarette smoke and body odour and had a large purple nose. Nonetheless, he seemed pleasant.

"Ah, we're just going to meet a friend in Athlone."

"Is that so? It's nice to have friends. I'm just heading over to see a lady friend myself." He held out a beefy hand. "Dan's the name, Dan Tucker."

Matt noticed a few heads turn at this, but he allowed his hand to be squeezed. David, who was listening with an expression of disapproval from the other side of the aisle, put a warning finger to his lips before taking his phone from his pocket.

"They have Wi-Fi on the bus," David announced, as he began scanning the Internet.

"Indeed they have," said the old man. "I never use the thing myself; dangerous it is, if you ask me. Do you use it... what did you say your name was again?"

"Matt O'Connor," Matt said.

"Well, that's a famous name now, isn't it? I suppose you know all about the Internet, surfing and that other thing, the book face and the swype? You have all that at home, do you?"

Before Matt could reply, David leaned over. "Ask him how his toothache is?"

"What?" Matt asked.

"How's your toothache, Mr Tucker?" said David. "The lyrics of the song are here on the Internet. It says Dan Tucker combed his hair with a wagon wheel and died from a toothache in his heel. That's not your real name, is it?"

"Ah be gob, ye're on to me all right," answered the old man, looking over at David. "You're the cuter of the two. I was only trying to teach your friend here a little lesson. Did your mother never warn you about talking to strangers?" he said to Matt.

With that, the man took an aged wallet from his pocket and showed them the badge that was displayed inside it. He explained that he was a retired police detective and that his name was Gabriel McNally.

The lady beside David joined the conversation.

"Don't mind him lads. He's always doing that. Our Gaybo still hasn't cottoned on to the fact that he's retired. Here, why don't I swap places with Matt O'Connor? Then you fellows can enjoy your trip without Sherlock Holmes there interrogating you."

"Ha!" said Gabriel McNally. "It works every time; she always sits beside me eventually. But you two are proper young gentlemen. Listen, if you ever need a retired detective, you know where to come, and you young Matt, take a leaf out of your friend's book when it comes to playing cute."

"I will." Matt agreed, moving over to join David.

When they reached Athlone, the weather was wet and dull. The two boys said goodbye to their new-found bus friends, before making their way to the chipper for lunch. While they waited for their food, David connected to the Wi-Fi and loaded Matt's PenChat account. When they had selected Noname101's name, they opened the section that contained his details.

"There's the address," pointed out Matt.

"Why would anyone put their address up on PenChat like that?" David asked.

"It's private, or supposed to be. Just like a private setting on Facebook or Scratch."

"That's what you think. Anyway do you think it's legit?"

"Let's go to 202 Valley Place and find out. We have two hours before we're supposed to be meeting him."

As they ate, Matt and David used the maps app on David's phone to find Noname101's housing estate and planned the best route. They decided to take an early exit off the Dublin road and to approach the last row of houses on the estate from the thick cover of the trees that ran along the railway track to the rear.

An hour later, the boys were in position, crouched low behind an ivy-covered hedge, watching Noname's house.

It was the last house on the row, one half of two semi-detached, partially red-brick houses whose gardens looked much the worse for wear. Unlike the other neatly kept houses, these two seemed sadly lacking in any kind of care and had no dividing wall between them. Outside, there were three rubbish bins, piled up and overflowing. It was obvious that they hadn't been emptied in a very long time. A blue Ford Transit van was parked in the weedy driveway.

"Are you sure this is the right place?" Matt asked. "It doesn't look the way Noname described it."

"Now, you're finally getting the picture. Noname is not a kid like us. He might not even be a kid at all. He could be some kind of snoop. Or worse."

"You're paranoid, David. He'll turn out to be perfectly normal, just like us."

"You mean normal as in mitching from school and spying on people who might turn out to be really bad ass criminals or something!" David laughed.

"I'm beginning to wonder what we're really doing here in broad daylight. But we've come this far... I suppose we have to see it through, just like real detectives."

The boys watched the house for any sign of activity, careful to make sure no one was watching them.

After a few minutes, David broke the silence. "You know what we were saying about Noname being different. He's not too unlike us, in a way."

"What do you mean?"

"You know, sometimes, people can be different. People like you. You know, like when you talk online. Different from your normal, real-life self, I mean."

"No, I'm not. I'm always me, Matt O'Connor."

"Crap. No one is. My dad says that people behave differently when they think they're anonymous. Not the same as when they have to face up to people, look them in the eye."

Their conversation was interrupted by a slight movement of a curtain in an upstairs bedroom. They both noticed it.

"Are you ready to take this to the next level?" said David intently.

"Yeah, go for it!"

David opened Matt's PenChat account and typed a message. 'Are you at home or in school?'

Just as he did this, someone appeared at an upstairs window and opened it before disappearing from view.

'Home,' the message came back.

'Did you skive off school?' David typed back.

'Yeah. Are you coming to Athlone?'

'No. That's why I'm sending you this. Got caught by the principal. Have detention.'

No reply came. The boys waited. Suddenly the figure appeared again at the window. His features were not clear to Matt and David, but they could see that it was a man. He was lighting a cigarette; plumes of blue smoke drifted out into the damp air. The man retreated.

A message came. 'Aw, bummer. Don't worry. We can catch up again.'

The man appeared at the window once again. This time, he was talking on his phone.

A few minutes later, an old, silver BMW pulled up outside the house. The two men in the car didn't get out. Instead, the driver's window was wound down. The man from upstairs emerged and limped to the driver's door, bending down to talk to him. The occupants of the car weren't visible from where the boys were positioned, but both of them had a clear view of the man facing them. Something about the uneven gait gave Matt his first clue. Then, the truth dawned on him as the man straightened up.

"It... it can't be!" he exclaimed.

"What? What is it?"

Somewhere deep in Matt's brain, things were beginning to make sense. "It's Ricky Moseley!"

"Are you one hundred per cent sure?"

"Yes... I'm sure."

***

Lost in a daze, Matt and David made their way back to the bus stop. The rain had got heavier, so they slipped under the shelter and stared at the drops of water pelting down in front of them.

"Hey," David pointed, "isn't that Gabriel McNally?"

"Come on!" he ordered.

They pushed past heavily laden shoppers who registered their disapproval.

"Hey!"

"Stop skipping!"

"I was here first!"

"You young hooligans!"

Finally the two boys found their way into a seat across the aisle from Gabriel. The woman was gone. Now he held a small girl in his arms.

"Hello again," he said, eyeing their empty hands, "how was your shopping trip?"

"Um... "

"Not enough money," improvised David rapidly, "Owww!"

As she pushed her way up the central aisle, a lady had stepped on David's protruding foot. He jumped up in pain, and loose change spilled out of his jacket pockets.

"Not enough money, eh?" Gabriel asked, with a touch of sarcasm.

"Who's that?" Matt rapidly changed the subject, gesturing at the girl, who was about two years old. Matt thought she looked dainty, petite and very fragile, especially in the big man's cradling grip, like thin china or crystal.

"This is my granddaughter, Rose. But don't change the subject. What were you really doing in Athlone?"

The boys exchanged glances. David nodded.

"Tell him."

"Okay," began Matt. "It's like this…"

Matt explained to Gabriel that they had skipped off school to visit his computer penpal. He pointed out that they had changed their minds and decided to go home instead.

"All right," Gabriel smiled. "But remember, having an anonymous contact can be dangerous."

"I know," said Matt.

The bus ride was very enjoyable. Little Rose had taken a great liking to Matt, and she wouldn't let him out of her sight. When they arrived back in Tullamore and were preparing to alight from the bus, Gabriel pressed a calling card into Matt's hand.

"Be careful, all right?" He said quietly. "I know more about you than you know."

"I'll try to be careful," Matt promised, confused by this strange warning.

"And remember, if you need anything, anything at all, be sure to get in touch with me."

"Thank you very much." Matt waved goodbye to Rose. She giggled and waved back.

- 16 -

BLUEJACKING

I n Matt's bedroom, later on that evening, the two boys discussed the situation with Ricky Moseley.

"Matt," said David, "what if we hack this guy's phone?"

"What do you mean?"

"I mean we could upload a Trojan onto it and wirelessly monitor his calls and texts. You can read them using a program on the computer."

"That would be great, if it's possible."

"Look it up on YouTube," suggested David, pointing at the computer.

Mr Freckles was perched on the edge of the desk. His eyes followed Matt as the boy walked over and hit the power button on the computer.

Be wary, young Matthew. Those who eavesdrop rarely like what they hear.

Shut up and keep your big fat nose out of my business Pinocchio, Matt fired back mentally.

He clicked on the YouTube icon on his desktop and typed 'how to wirelessly upload a Trojan onto a phone,' into the search bar.

There were ten results.

David stared at the results in amazement. "Wouldn't you think most of these videos would have been removed?"

"Yeah, I'd say so." Matt clicked on the video link.

"Quick Matt, get a pen. We need to write this down."

"Ok."

Matt grabbed a piece of paper and a pen from his desk and began to take notes.

Step 1: Create a new contact.

Step 2: Send Message.

Step 3: Upload virus onto message.

Step 4: Get within 10 metres of victim.

Step 5: Press send via Bluetooth.

"I didn't think hacking was so easy," said Matt. "But how do we get the virus? It just shows how to upload it."

"I don't know, but I think I can use my coding skills." David looked thoughtful.

"What do you mean?"

"I go to programming classes in Saint Mary's Youth Centre. I think I can copy this and make a custom virus so we can wirelessly listen to his calls and read his texts."

"That's great! Are you sure you can do that?"

"I'm sure," David said confidently.

After checking other tutorials, David found the source of the online demonstrations and slowly began to import small lines of code. Soon there were rows of squiggles, dashes and symbols that meant nothing to Matt. David slowly began to assemble them into what he explained was the code for a Trojan virus.

"Cool," he said finally, once he was satisfied. "Matt, did you get all that?"

"I haven't the faintest idea what it all means, but if you say it will work, then I believe you."

"If it does work, you can call me Professor Messer."

"But how are we going to send the virus to Ricky's phone?"

"I'll upload it to the Internet from the computer. Then we can download it to a phone and send it from there."

"Whose phone?"

David looked thoughtful. "We can't use mine. My dad checks it all the time. He has a program on his computer that lets him see what

I'm doing whenever I'm connected to the Internet."

"Bummer!"

"It's okay," said David. "He's just looking out for me. Does your sister have a phone? We could ask her for a loan of it."

Matt and David went to Rachel's door and knocked.

"Come in. If that's you, Matt, I'm busy."

Matt walked straight into his sister's room, but David stayed in the hall.

"Matt, I'll stay out here and wait," he said, looking awkwardly at his feet.

"Ok, suit yourself."

Rachel, who was sitting at her dressing table, applying mascara to her eyelashes, groaned loudly when Matt asked her if he could borrow her phone."

"Of course not, idiot. I need it to text Derek. I have a date with him this evening. Now go away, won't you? I have to get ready.

Matt closed the door a little harder than necessary.

"You're welcome," shouted Rachel.

"Let's do it," said Matt decisively to David. "All we need is a mobile phone."

- 17 -

PRESSURE

I t was a cold bleak day, and though the sun may have been shining somewhere in the world, none of its rays reached the abandoned construction site. In one of the little office huts, which had flowery curtains in the window in a feeble attempt to introduce warmth and pleasantry to the cold and damp, a man sat reading the *Sun* newspaper. His huge bulky frame was spilled into an ugly, orange swivel chair. The only sounds were the monotonous pulse of the clock on the corrugated iron wall and the occasional rustle of paper. The man's attention was momentarily drawn to the sloshing sound of a jeep ploughing through the mud and puddles of the yard outside. Then he continued reading, sipping from the plastic cup of bitter black coffee that might once have been warm.

Ricky Moseley stormed in, disturbing the peace of the afternoon. "This has got to end, boss. I'm sick to death of that mewling, idiotic bitch and those whining brats of hers! I don't know what O'Connor saw in her."

The boss didn't even raise his eyes from the newspaper. "Stop your moaning, you weakling. Get your job done."

"But I'm tired of trying to squeeze information out of the boy."

"Listen, Moseley, we've got to put an end to all this! You're with that woman to try and flush out O'Connor. And why aren't I seeing any headlines in that paper about a mother who is too depressed to mind her own kids and has to put them in care? The sort of thing Ronan O'Connor would notice? That woman isn't supposed to be looking after them anymore, Moseley."

"I'm doing the best I can," rasped Moseley. "I'm feeding her Prozac by the bucketful. She shouldn't even be able to get out of bed, but she seems to be getting more energetic by the day."

"She's falling for you," the large man sneered. "Can't you make her overdose? Slip her something when she's drunk! At this rate, we'll never get O'Connor to make a move. We simply have to bring him out in the open. And the next time, we'll finish the job."

Moseley was getting angrier by the second. He kicked over a rusty metal paper bin beside the desk.

"That's more like it," said his boss. "Apply a little of that aggression to the O'Connor woman. The Mr Nice Guy act isn't working. We have to finish the job we started seven bloody years ago. Remember that scumbag wounded you and murdered Gino. It's time for payback."

Involuntarily, Moseley's hand crept up to his thigh. He still had the scar from where O'Connor had shot him all that time ago.

"That piece of trash murdered one of my men and burned him like a lump of turf. Have you forgotten your time in the Joy so fast?"

The boss's voice retreated into the background as Moseley's mind was swamped with memories he had long tried to forget; images of dark corridors, of barred doors and slop buckets.

"Are you even listening? What did I just say?"

"Um, seven bloody years, boss. Time for payback," Ricky answered through gritted teeth.

"Wrong. I moved on from that to tell you that if you don't get this job done, I'll call in someone else. Do you understand?"

Ricky understood. He felt his hand begin to shake. *If only I could take some right now,* he thought.

"Wouldn't it be possible to make her overdose, or something like that? Couldn't be too hard, not if you've got her sufficiently charmed up. Make her dinner and add a special ingredient. You have plenty of *special ingredients,* from what I hear."

"You heard wrong. I'm not using. Honest, I'm not." Both of Ricky's hands were shaking now. He shoved them into his pockets, out of sight.

"I don't care what you do when this is finished, Moseley. Right now, I just want you to flush that dirty rat out of whatever hole he's in, and I don't want any Guards onto us, do you hear? He's close, I know he is. It's time for us to take what we've earned."

Ricky gave a nervous chuckle. "No worries, boss. I have a nice little plan for the daughter, and there'll be an ambulance at the house for Colette before I'm finished with her."

As quickly as possible, Ricky made his exit.

As soon as the boss heard the engine start up, he folded his newspaper and set it down neatly on the desk before reaching for the telephone and dialling a number.

"Trent?" he said quietly, "I'll need you to bring your boys in. Moseley's got some kind of plan for the daughter and he's going to poison the mother. But, if those two little stunts don't work, we move next week – with or without Moseley."

- 18 -

PEPPER SPRAY

All through school, Matt couldn't concentrate. His recent visit to Durrow Abbey had caused questions about his father to whizz around his head. *Where has he been? What does he look like now? Did he do some of the things people claimed he did? Will I live up to his expectations? Will he live up to mine?*

"Matt, Matt!" David whispered from behind him.

"Matthew O'Connor?" called out the geography teacher, Mr Hogan.

"What?" Matt raised his head. All around the class, people were sniggering and laughing.

The teacher raised a hand, calling for silence. "What did I just say?"

"Well, um, I wasn't paying attention."

"If you're not going to take part in class, Mr O'Connor, I will have to assume that you want more work to do at home. That will be extra homework, questions A, B and C, for everybody tonight!"

Matt swore under his breath.

"What was that?" Mr Hogan raised his eyebrows. "A profanity? I hope not. I'll have you know that any misconduct will be discussed at the parent-teacher meetings, and that applies to all of you."

Luckily, the bell rang at that moment. Matt packed his bag, trying to ignore the dirty looks that were being cast in his direction. As he left the classroom, he heard the familiar sound of Billy and his gang. They were waiting for him.

"So Matt, I see you have your costume for the Halloween party!" called Billy.

His gang laughed appreciatively.

"No," answered Matt, "this face isn't scary enough. I'm going as you, just to be really petrifying."

Several members of the gang laughed in spite of themselves.

"Shut up, goons," said Billy. "Think you're a comedian, do you?" he asked Matt.

Matt didn't answer. He walked away, trying to keep his head high.

That evening, Matt thought about this conversation as he sat at the kitchen table, eating a bowl of soup. He sighed. Even Rachel's lovely soup couldn't cheer him up; he was so sick of Pimple Face and his cronies. Eventually, he gave up and, leaving the bowl on the counter, went upstairs. Kicking off his shoes, he lay down on his bed, feeling hot tears building in his eyes.

He didn't want to play computer games. He didn't want to do his homework. Even the comfort of talking to Noname 101 was gone, now he had discovered that it was just Ricky Moseley in disguise. Matt felt sick when he thought of everything he had told Noname, believing that he was chatting to a friend. He pulled the covers over his head, feeling queasy at the thought of facing Pimple Face in school every day on top of all his other problems. It was just too much.

Think Matt, think! He clutched his head and squeezed it as if he could get ideas to pop out of his mouth. Suddenly, an idea came. *Mace! Pepper spray even. I'm gonna give it back to those bullies.* Matt considered. *But where am I going to get pepper spray?*

Mr Freckles was leaning against the computer. Matt jumped into his chair, pushed the dummy to one side, and began to Google 'How to make pepper spray.'

Matthew, violence is never the answer!

"Be quiet, you stupid dummy! What do you know?" Matt continued searching. "Nope, nope, ah!" Matt clicked the third link down and it took him to the instructions. He looked at the ingredients.

"Peppers? Sure. Black pepper? Fine. Water? I can do that. A container capable of spraying? That could be a problem."

Matt opened a drawer and started searching through it for something useful.

"An inhaler? Perfect! He picked up one of his plastic inhalers. *I can probably use a syringe or something,* he thought.

Be cautious, young Matthew. The bully you speak of might give you a taste of your own medicine. Your pain could be doubled!

"Shut up!" Matt dashed downstairs and gathered the ingredients.

Step one, crush the peppers. Matt grabbed the bowl meant for crushing and mincing spice and threw in some peppers. Once he had crushed them, he heated some water, grabbed a big bowl and placed it on the counter. *Add water, four shakes of black pepper and hey presto!* He grabbed a syringe and sucked some up. Using a knife, he made a tiny hole in the inhaler and injected the mix into it.

"Perfect!"

Matt got up the following day feeling happier than usual. He packed his bag, schoolbooks, lunch and the inhaler full of pepper spray, checking twice to make sure it was the right one.

He was eager for his morning classes to end, each minute felt like an hour. Finally the bell rang. *Lunch time, perfect time to test my bully repellent!*

Matt walked out of the door and headed in the direction of his locker where, true to form, Pimple Face was loitering with intent. When he saw Matt heading towards him, he smirked.

"Hey, Mattie, what are you doing? You want to go to your locker? I can help you get in."

"I won't need your help," replied Matt, trying to look as tough as possible.

"Are you getting smart with me, O'Connor?" Pimple Face looked around to check that nobody was nearby and raised a fist.

Before Pimple Face could throw a punch, Matt yanked out the inhaler and sprayed. Billy Dinglefitz covered his eyes and fell to the floor crying.

"What's happening to me?" he screeched.

Shocked at the effectiveness of his spray, Matt leaned down to the bully. "It... it should wear off soon," he said, offering a helping hand.

Pimple Face tried to lunge away from Matt, only to bang his head on the corner of a locker. "Christ, O'Connor, if you did this to me, make it go away, please!"

"My name is Matt. And I want you to stop what you're doing to me."

"Make it go away, Matt, please!"

"You're going to need this," said Matt, grabbing a bottle of water out of his backpack. "Here, let me," he said, gently splashing it into his tormentor's eyes.

Rubbing his eyes, Billy stood up. He blinked and looked at Matt.

"What was that stuff?" he asked.

"Just something I made." Matt picked up Billy's backpack from the ground and held it out to him.

"Are you two boys all right there?" a passing teacher asked.

"Yes, Miss," both boys chorused, as if the line had been rehearsed.

When the teacher was out of earshot, Billy turned to Matt. He wore a sheepish expression. He shrugged his shoulders in an awkward fashion as if he were trying to say something that just wouldn't come out.

Finally he said, "Listen Matt. I've been pretty rotten to you. I shouldn't have been so mean. Here, do you want this?" He rummaged in his bag and produced a phone, which he pushed in Matt's direction.

Matt lifted his two hands up and backed away from the phone as if touching it would contaminate him. "I can't take it. You don't have to give me that."

"No, take it. The phone shop will only give me twenty for it, anyway. My dad got me a new one. I really want you to take it. Go on. I'm trying to apologise here. I know you don't have a phone."

"How do you know I don't already have one?"

"You don't wanna know."

"What do you mean?"

"If you had a phone, we would have made your life hell."

Matt stared at Billy, not knowing how to respond. Looking shiftily around, Billy motioned for Matt to move to the side area of the lockers as he opened the screen on his own phone. "I can barely see," he said as he did so. "Are you sure that stuff will wear off?"

"It will."

Billy began to show Matt pictures of him and David. Their heads had been superimposed onto other bodies and other images.

"Look," Billy said, "before you see all this crap, I am going to apologise again. We have pictures of you and David on a site. Lanky Murphy photoshopped them to make it look like you two guys were... well you know, a happily married couple and other things," he laughed, before checking himself again. "I didn't like it, I swear, really I didn't. I mean, it's one thing to give someone a bit of a slagging or a push or something... messing like. But this is a whole different load of mean crap. I'll make him take it down before anyone sees it apart from us."

"You're right. It's not nice. It's all right for you. You have loads of friends. So far, I only have one and this is what you would do to him. How long is it up?"

"I swear that stuff isn't anywhere yet. I'll talk to Lanky. If he did anything with this, I'll kill him personally. That's why I want to give you this." He held the phone out again. "Please."

Very gingerly, Matt accepted the gift.

Billy smiled awkwardly, as if his facial muscles were not used to the action.

"I have the charger at home," he said. "You'll have to go to the phone shop. He'll sell you a sim card, and you'll be in business. Are we good?" He held out a hand.

Tentatively, Matt shook it.

"I thought I was never gonna see again," gasped Billy as they walked to the canteen. "You scared the crap out of me. How did you do it?"

"That's top secret, I'm afraid."

"Okay. Cool. Listen, I'm sorry again, okay?"

"Okay."

The two boys parted company at the entrance to the canteen. As he watched Billy walk over to join his gang members at their table, Matt didn't know whether to laugh or cry with relief. He examined the phone in his hand. It was an iPhone. He decided to raid his piggy bank as soon as he got home from school. He needed to get to the phone shop to buy a SIM card and some credit.

Thoughts of visiting the phone shop went out of Matt's mind when he got home, however. He was shocked to see Rachel sitting at the kitchen table with the scrapbook Matt had removed from Durrow Abbey open in front of her. She looked at up him, and he could see that she had been crying.

"Where did you get this?" she demanded.

"Have you read it all?"

"I just started, but Matt, it's all about us!"

Rachel read aloud from the scrapbook.

TRAGEDY STRIKES O'CONNOR HOUSEHOLD

Following the tragic scenes at Durrow Abbey on the 13th of February, further tragedy was heaped on the O'Connor family with the grim discovery of charred remains of a middle-aged man. Sadly, initial signs at the scene point to the remains being those of Ronan O'Connor. His wedding ring, wallet, watch and other personal items were found close by. His body was originally discovered by the Tullamore fire brigade beside the burned out stables to the rear of Durrow Abbey. Dr Yvonne Warren, the state pathologist, established burning as the cause of death, although bullets were found lodged in the torso and leg. The remains have been brought to Tullamore General Hospital, and a full post-mortem will give more information on the events surrounding his death. "It's truly terrible that this level of evil can be found in the likes of Durrow, a beautiful country area," said Police Chief Johnson. Chief Johnson has issued an appeal to the public for information. Mr O'Connor's wife, Colette, 32, and his two children, Rachel, aged 8, and Matthew, 5, are being cared for at a secret location following their dramatic rescue on the night of the raid at their home. They are said to be in good health. A spokesperson for the police force told this reporter that they are badly shaken by the fateful events of Thursday night last and are receiving counselling. This further sad development will intensify their burden of grief.

"This is incredible," said Rachel. "I don't understand."

"Read the next one," Matt said.

BIZARRE TWIST IN DURROW TALE

Following the discovery of charred human remains at Durrow Abbey on the night of 13th of February last, this newspaper reported that they belonged to Mr Ronan O'Connor, owner of Durrow Abbey. The remains, which were subsequently removed for examination by the State Pathologist, Dr Yvonne Warren three weeks ago, are now believed to be those of another man who is known to the police. DNA testing has revealed that they are those of Gino Wogan, a known criminal who has been on the run from police and is wanted for a number of violent crimes, including armed robbery. Wogan is believed to be part of a gang that also included Ricky Molloy, who was wounded at the scene and is currently in police custody. Strangely, nothing belonging to Wogan was found in the vicinity of the body. However, many items of Mr O'Connor's were discovered on or about the corpse. These included his wedding ring which was fused onto the finger of the deceased. It now appears that Mr O'Connor may have tried to give the impression that it was he who was murdered in the woods of Durrow. This bizarre twist in events should come as somewhat of a consolation to Colette O'Connor and her family, but it is too early to say, according to police sources, whether or not Mr O'Connor has survived the sad events of the 13th of February. Police are continuing to appeal for witnesses and information relating to the events.

Rachel stood up and walked over to the window.

"I don't believe this," she said. "Why would he do that? How come we were never told the full story? This just isn't fair, Matt. I'm going to talk to Mum. Tell her what we know."

"That Dad is alive?"

"Yeah, that he's alive. Can you believe all that nonsense she fed us all those years? Waiting in bed for some non-existent pay out from his insurance... lying there feeling sorry for herself. It's no wonder people picked on you, Matt. You had no one to stand up for you. And they both should have been there for you."

"You were there for me, Rach."

"I was a poor substitute for real parents. I am really mad. I'm mad with both of them. What were they thinking?"

"What'll we do now?"

"When she gets home from work, we'll show this to her, and make her explain it."

***

In spite of her simmering anger, Rachel managed to cook chicken goujons with roast potatoes, vegetables and instant gravy for dinner that evening. Matt set the table in the dining room and lit a fire in the grate, hoping to soften the impending confrontation. It worked, to some extent. Colette was delighted when she returned home from work. They sat and ate in awkward silence, though.

When they had finished eating, Rachel picked up the scrapbook, which she had left on the chair beside her, and placed it in front of their mother, opened at the article she had read earlier.

"Where did...?" Colette began, recoiling when she saw the headline.

"Matt found it in Durrow Abbey." Rachel answered the unspoken question. "We have just one question for you, Mum."

"Now wait a minute. I thought I said… "

"You wanted to keep us away from there so we wouldn't find out what really happened. That's why you moved us all up to Naas, so you could shield us from the truth, the truth being that our father is still alive."

"Now, Rachel. You don't have the right to speak to me like that. "

Good time for me to stay out of this one, Matt thought.

A splendid idea for once, Matthew, a voice in the distance agreed.

Rachel was now on a roll; seven years of caring, carrying the weight of worry and often the responsibility of an adult; of comforting her mother, looking after both herself and her brother, seemed to be coming out now in her words of anger.

"Mum, I didn't mind helping you with housework, helping Matt with his homework, moving house three times, caring for your mother when she was sick, and you too when you were under the weather, as you put it. All of that was no problem. I would do it again ten times over. But what I do mind is being lied to. I mind that very much."

Colette was defeated. The last remark took the words out of her mouth. She stared at both of her children, pain evident in a face that looked older than her thirty-nine years.

After a long pause, she began to speak. "On the night of the 13th of February, my life, all our lives, fell apart. It started when the alarm was set off by a camera sensor at the front gate. That was before the power was cut to the main house. The back-up generator kicked in long enough for us to get a few things together. I got you two, and your father, you know what he took. He made me get into the basement that led to the tunnel, but he refused to come with us, saying that he would meet us at the other end, where we always kept your grandfather's old Mercedes as a backup."

"Was he trying to draw the raiders away?" Matt asked.

"I don't know," Colette answered. "He didn't come out at the stable yard end of the tunnel. The gang must have known about the escape route, because they seemed to get out of the house really quickly, and one of them must have started a fire in the vicinity of the stables. That would have been easy enough with all the hay and so on. What happened next was... is still a blur. When we emerged from our rat hole, the raiders were firing shots at your father and chasing after him into the night. One of them must have spotted us. They bundled us into the back of a van."

"Did they want to trade us for the Crown Jewels?"

"Possibly. But anyway, they were foiled by the police. We were abandoned and they made their getaway in another car they had, which was later found burnt out somewhere in Athlone."

"But... what happened to Dad?" Matt asked, trembling slightly.

"He had this ancient revolver with him. He hit one of the thieves, wounding him, and the man did time in jail. He killed another and..." she hesitated, holding something back, before continuing on a different tack. "But your father must have been hurt too. How bad, I'll never know."

Colette's eyes were watery. She put her hand briefly over her face before she continued. "Do you both remember the little prayer mound we built for your father, at the rockery, on the sunny bank?"

They both nodded slowly.

She went on. "About a month after the raid, I began to believe that he would come back. We were forbidden from going back to the house, apart from collecting a few clothes and some possessions. You wanted to look for your father. Matt, you kept looking for Mr Tickles. To try and make you realise that your father was gone, we made the little altar. It was March and we transplanted snowdrops and daffodils and you left pictures and food. Can you imagine how heartbroken I was, looking at my two little children and knowing that it was possibly all a lie... that their father was out there somewhere? Then, that summer, we cut flowers from the prayer mound and threw them in the stream to say goodbye. You both remember?"

Rachel was quieter now when she spoke. "But we never dealt with the truth, Mum. You might have, but Matt and I didn't. We were allowed to grow up in some kind of limbo as far as Dad was concerned. Surely you knew something? You could have given us some hope of seeing him again. You didn't have the right to tell us he was dead, when you knew he wasn't."

"I wish you could say that to your father. But he isn't here is he?"

"I did say it to him," said Rachel. "And yes, he is here now."

"What? What do you mean?"

"Do you mean you've actually seen him?" Matt asked Rachel in astonishment.

Colette stood up, raised her hands. "No. I'm not hearing this. It's not happening again. I can't take this."

She went over to the kitchen counter and began to make her usual after-dinner coffee.

"That's a good sign," Matt whispered, only to get another of his sister's 'do-you-want-me-to-start-on-you' looks.

When Colette came back to the table, coffee mug in hand, she seemed more composed. "So you've been in contact with your father, Rachel? When were you going to tell me?"

"I'm telling you now. And Matt is telling you that we might possibly be in danger again, but I'm not so sure about his information... most of it is coming from a person who talks to a wooden doll."

Colette gave a steely look in Matt's direction. "I have made a lot of mistakes since your father disappeared, but hooking up with him again is not another one I intend to make. For month on endless month after he left, I waited for him. I kept watch day and night, exhausted every possible connection, every avenue. I must have looked out of a thousand windows!"

Matt and Rachel were stunned into silence. Colette had never before opened up to them about her own grief.

She continued. "So forget about the lovely reunion. Sorry, Matt but that is not going to happen. Look, you two are the most important part of my life right now. What you have done for me, Rachel! I'll never be able to tell you how close I was to giving up... both of you have helped put me back on my feet, and I'll answer all your questions whenever I can, but please, please drop this whole thing. There is no danger, and this reunion is not going to happen."

"But... " Matt began.

"Leave it, Matt!" Rachel interrupted him. "That's enough for now."

"Thanks Rach. Thanks for such a lovely dinner... you too, Mattie.

Now guys could I please have a hug? Please?" Their mother held out her arms.

Slowly, both her children wrapped themselves around their mother and just stood there... for the longest time.

- 19 -

ACTION

After school the next day, Matt and David sat in front of the computer going over the final details of their plan to get the Trojan virus onto Moseley's phone. First David had taken Matt on a tour of the Snapchat grabs he had taken from Lanky Murphy's handy work. Matt couldn't believe the trouble Lanky had gone to just to make fun of both of them. David though, was taking it all in his stride.

"My dad thought it was quite funny," he explained, "once he finished threatening to murder Lanky and everybody belonging to him. Instead we just packaged it all up in a neat little folder and sent it to the principal, the police youth officer and the other boys' parents. Dad followed all the messages up with phone calls".

"Wow. What did they say?"

"Apologised mostly. Murphy's dad asked us not to tell the school. Billy's dad said that he was going to kill his son."

"What did your dad say?"

"He told them the truth, that a file was gone to the school and the police. And that the rest was up to them."

"Wow, David, you knew all this was going on, and you still hung around with me. That means a lot."

"I didn't have a choice. If I backed down on a friend because of a bunch of idiots, my dad would never forgive me. He says that's not the way we act in our family. He went on his usual lecture about our family motto which is "Esto Fideles" or something like that. Whatever it means, it calls on us to be loyal and true to our friends. So here I am, Mattie, ready to go to the ends of the Earth with you... well to Athlone at least," David laughed.

"Aw shucks, man. We can do it," Matt said, giving his friend a friendly punch.

"Our plan is great, but how will we actually make it work?" David asked.

"You said we have to get within ten metres of Moseley's house and connect to his Internet router."

"Yeah, just like that. You think Moseley is going to let us get that close?"

"How about his garden shed? Will that be close enough?"

"It might be. But the problem is getting there without being seen."

"We'll just have to try it and hope for the best," said Matt seriously.

"Well, I'm good with hardware. I can do it quickly," David pointed out. "We'll just go and find the right place to hide when we get there."

The next morning, the two boys arrived at Tullamore Comprehensive and went to assembly as before, taking great care to say good morning in their most cheerful voices to everyone they met on the way. They had soon left by the side exit and were on the 9.30 am bus to Athlone.

Matt and David were the only people on the bus this time. Almost as if to allay their anxiety about the task that lay ahead of them, they both tucked into their lunches. Soon the only noise that broke the silence between them was the sound made by the munching of crisps.

An hour later, the two boys were crouching down behind the wall opposite Moseley's house. A blue van parked in the driveway indicated that their target was probably at home.

"Creep," said Matt. "He was driving a red convertible when he collected my mother. He probably hired it to make himself look cool."

Checking that no one was about, they cautiously crept along the hedge that bordered the end of the road and entered Moseley's back garden. In no time at all, they were crouched among the rubbish in his garden shed. No sign of life came from the damp looking house.

"Looks like he's still asleep," Matt said.

"Right then. You know the drill. I've written a script. Open the terminal and type 'sudo./TrojanHack.sh.'"

"Hang on, hang on." Matt tapped swiftly at the phone's touchscreen. "Yeah, I have it. What's next?"

"Press enter!"

They watched anxiously as the message was sent to Ricky Moseley's phone number. Matt had copied it from his mother's list of contacts.

"Now, all we have to do is wait for the victim to open his lovely message from the brilliant Professor Messer," said David, in his best Einstein voice.

"Are you sure he won't suspect anything?"

"No way. He's never going to refuse five hundred euros' worth of treatment lotions for bald guys, is he?"

"It should at least get him curious." Matt tried to avoid laughing too loudly.

"Trojan is in place! Now all we have to do is wait."

Matt and David left the garden shed and made their way back along the hedge. Twenty minutes later, they were on the bus home. As it pulled up at the bus stop in Tullamore, a beep told them that Moseley had sent a text.

Matt opened it. 'I can't read it,' he said. "It's all squiggles."

"It's encrypted," said David. "Don't worry. We can read it using the program on your computer or if you forward it to my phone. Do that, quickly."

In seconds the message appeared on David's phone in its original form… 'I have the gear. Will use it next week.'

"What is he on about?" Matt was puzzled by the message.

"Gear. It sounds dangerous. But at least we are on to him. We are going to find out a lot more about this guy. Now following the excitement of your morning's adventures, let's get you back to the thrilling prospect of another scintillating lecture on the Renaissance from Mrs Gaughan."

"Sounds absolutely exhilarating," Matt said, reminding himself of his wooden friend, "but at least it's Friday."

***

Matt spent half the night looking out of the window, expecting to see Moseley's blue van prowling around his estate. When his alarm rang at eight o' clock, he decided to take the only course of action that might help. He would have to talk to Gabriel McNally. He searched through his school bag and eventually found the card with the address on it.

After a basic breakfast of tea and toast, Matt borrowed Rachel's bike once more and began his journey. Ten minutes later, he was ringing Gabriel McNally's doorbell. There was a long pause, but eventually the door was opened by a man with hair that was rather wet and uncombed. He was dressed in a dressing gown which Matt was sure was meant to be white, but was now more of a beige colour. McNally looked a bit annoyed at being disturbed so early on a Saturday morning.

"Um... hi Gabriel." Matt felt slightly awkward.

"Hello, Matt isn't it?" grumbled Gabriel. "Come on in."

Gabriel's home was rather cosy. The first thing Matt noticed was the sleek, black leather three-seater couch in front of a fire. A few briquettes were already burning in the grate.

"I like your house," said Matt.

"Thank you... But why come here at nine o' clock in the morning?"

"I'm very worried about something. I have a question that has been bothering me a lot, and I need to know the answer."

"Well why don't you just ask then?"

"What exactly is my dad charged with?"

"Right Matt, I think you're old enough to know. I'm afraid your dad is still wanted for manslaughter. I don't really think we need to go into much detail."

"No, please Gabriel, just tell me. I'm going to find out sooner or later."

Gabriel paused for a moment and then wandered over to the sink and poured himself a glass of water. "Can I get you anything Matt?" he asked, avoiding the question.

Matt shook his head and waited for an answer.

"I'm sorry to have to tell you, but your father chased and shot a gang member and then burned the corpse. He also shot and wounded another gang member who has spent the last six years of his life in jail. As far as I know, he is still in there. You have to understand that this was all in the heat of the moment. Any man would do what he did to protect his family."

"He killed someone?" Matt asked, the shock evident in his voice.

"I don't blame him," said Gabriel, "It was either kill or be killed. The gang members were armed. And if he was on the receiving end, he would have lost the crown jewels, and maybe you mightn't be here today. I think it's acceptable. But maybe he should have waited to face the jury. That's the part I'll never understand."

"Thanks for the information." Matt decided to tell Gabriel what he and David had done with Moseley's phone.

Gabriel looked worried. "Where are you keeping all this information you're getting from Moseley's phone?"

"On my computer," Matt explained.

"If that means what I think it means, you can't risk anyone finding out about what you've done. It could put you and your family in danger. I think you would be wise to hide the computer somewhere else."

Matt considered.

"How about Agatha's? She lives in the Gate Lodge at Durrow Abbey, and she knows all about the crime. Do you know her?"

Gabriel's wrinkled face broke into a smile.

"I do, indeed. That's not a bad idea at all. But how would she feel about it?" he asked.

"She has helped me a lot and I know I can count on her," Matt replied.

"Well if that's good enough for you, it's good enough for me. Do you want to call her from here?"

While Gabriel went to dress himself and get something to eat, Matt made arrangements over the phone with Agatha. He was relieved to hear her welcoming approval of his plan.

Gabriel picked up the car keys and a few minutes later, Matt was in the front passenger seat of Gabriel's car, having shoved the bike into the boot. They drove quickly to Matt's house. When they got there, he opened his front door as silently as possible and tiptoed up the stairs, trying not to disturb anyone. After much unplugging of cables, he was back in Gabriel's car with the computer on his lap.

***

"Well, hello there dears. Come in, come in! Would you like a cup of tea?" Agatha met them at the door. She was wearing an old housecoat and had her hair tightly done up in curlers.

"No thanks, Agatha," Matt answered. "I've brought a friend. He says he knows you."

"Well, Mr McNally, if it isn't yourself. You're welcome," she said, waving them in. "I have a spare room here that will do just perfectly!"

Agatha led them to an old room that looked like it hadn't been used in a hundred years. The corners were decorated with cobwebs and the red and gold carpet was covered with dust. The windows were blocked with overgrown plants and shrubbery, but Agatha had already gone to the trouble of lighting a fire in the beautiful ornate fireplace. The room was quite dim, and no natural light came through the windows. The old woman dusted off a light switch and flicked on the light. Matt heard a distinct crackling sound before the room was flooded with light by a beautiful chandelier hanging from the ceiling.

"This will do the trick!" Matt said as he placed the computer on a rugged oak table. Gabriel handed him the set of cables and the mouse, and Matt plugged everything in and switched on the machine. Using his new phone as a Wi-Fi hotspot, he connected the computer to the Internet and double clicked the file on his computer labelled 'BLUEJACKING.' It opened a folder which contained transcripts of phone texts.

Mission complete, Matt thought to himself, smiling. "We're going to leave this here now," he said to Agatha. You don't have to worry about it. Just leave it alone. I'll come back tomorrow to check on it."

"Don't worry Matt, I will look after your com... com..." Agatha glanced down at a scrap of paper that she had written notes on, "computer."

Matt and Gabriel left soon afterwards, and Agatha returned to the kitchen and made herself a cup of tea. "Ahhh…" she said, "nothing like a good mug o' scald".

She carried her cup back to the spare room and examined the out-of-place machine that lay in front of her. She looked for the on button. "Hmmm… this can't be more complicated than my kettle."

In spite of Matt's warning, Agatha fiddled with the keyboard. A message appeared on the screen, asking for a password. Agatha went back into the hall, picked up her phone handset and dialled.

Matt's weary voice answered. "Hello."

"Hello, young Matt," she replied, "What is the password for your C.P.?"

"P.C? The password is MOConnor5 but..."

"Thank you my dear," Agatha said, putting the phone back into its cradle and returning to the spare room. She settled down into a comfy chintz armchair facing the computer and began to type. A new message appeared. 'Would you like to change this password,? it asked.

"Oh, that would be nice," said Agatha. "That one is much too hard to remember."

She typed in: FROLICKING IN FLOWERS.

Much better!

Agatha peered closely at the screen. *It's very grubby,* she thought, noticing the finger marks on it. She went into the kitchen. "I know it's around here somewhere." She got onto a stool, reached up into the small, dusty cupboard and pulled out a half empty bottle of Windowlene. "Got it!" Agatha grabbed a cloth and returned to the computer. She sprayed the screen and after giving it a good rub she stood back to admire her handiwork. "Perfect!"

After ensuring that the screen was sparkling, Agatha attempted to open the programme that was spying on Moseley, but to no avail. *Come on, Angie you can conquer this... this... cat's melodeon. Use that old noggin. You must have to use the pedal.*

Some time later, Agatha rang Matt again.

"Hello?" he answered.

"Hello, Matteen, I'm just having a spot o' bother with this puter of yours... maybe you should come over. The pedal is not working properly."

"Pedal?"

"Yes."

"Aaah... it's okay," he said, "you don't have to do anything. There's no rush. I'll have a look next time I'm over."

"That's all right so. And by the way, I cleaned your screen."

Matt sounded alarmed. "With what?"

"Windowlene, silly!"

"I'll be right over!"

"Alright. Bysie bye now!"

Within minutes, Matt was at Agatha's door, sweat plastering his forehead.

"Good afternoon young man. Would you like a biscuit? Tea?"

Matt shook his head. *Doesn't she ever have proper meals? Or is it all tea and biscuits?* He went into the spare room and examined the computer.

"Where's the mouse?" he asked.

"Mouse!" shrieked Agatha, hitching up her long skirts. She ran into the hall and grabbed a sweeping brush. "I'll get him. Find the cat for me, will you?"

"No!" said Matt, exasperated, "A computer mouse!"

"Oh! Are they friendly?"

"Oh dear," Matt muttered under his breath, "This!" he replied picking the mouse up off the floor.

"The pedal?"

"No, it's not. It's a mouse."

"But it's a pedal."

"No! This is a computer mouse!" said Matt, getting a little frustrated at Agatha's stupidity.

"It's alive?"

"No Agatha, it's not a real mouse."

"Then why is it called a mouse?"

Matt put his head in his hand, "Just take my word for it, okay."

"Fine," Agatha pursed her lips. "Silly boy," she muttered to herself.

"Agatha, you are not, I repeat, not, allowed to use this computer. Is that understood?"

"Fine, I'll stick with my kettle. I can work the kettle."

"It has two buttons," Matt said, unimpressed.

"I know," Agatha replied proudly.

"Look, just wait until Mr McNally, David and I come over."

"Detective McNally? Oh, he's a nice fella. A bit of a codder, but harmless all the same."

Matt returned to the door, and climbed back on his bike. "Okay. Agatha I have to go now. My school is having a Halloween party tonight. Remember, no touching the PC."

"Alright, would you like a biscuit before you go?"

"No thanks. Bye."

"Goodbye."

- 20 -

KIDNAPPED

C olette was sitting in front of a mirror putting the finishing touches to her make up. Her stomach rumbled as she heard a car pull into the driveway.

"He's here."

She braced herself, knowing that tonight was to be the last time she would see Ricky Moseley. After her recent conversation with Matt and Rachel, she had decided to put her children first. She walked to the front door, pushing in an earring as she went.

Moseley was standing on the doorstep.

"Colette," he said, "you look... stunning".

Colette glanced down at the slinky dress that she wore. It had been her favourite gift from Ronan.

"Oh, this old thing," she said with an airy laugh, "you must be joking."

"I'm not," he exclaimed as they walked into the kitchen. The lights were dimmed and the table had been set beautifully.

"Wow, you have the place looking lovely," said Moseley.

"Thanks," Colette said, laughing uneasily. There was something odd about Ricky this evening, she noticed. His gaze kept flicking away from her, as if he didn't want to catch her eye.

Moseley placed two carrier bags on a counter.

"You sit down. I'm going to make dinner, like I said, to make up for the hurtful comment I made the other night."

"If you're sure?"

"I am."

Colette took a seat at the table.

"Now," said Moseley, rolling up his sleeves, "watch me make my family's world famous Gaelic sauce."

He started measuring out various ingredients, but out of the corner of her eye, Colette saw a battered old cookery book hidden beneath a teacloth. After a couple of minutes, he plucked a bottle of Tullamore Dew whiskey from one of the bags. "This is the best bit." He poured a large amount into a bowl, and then generous shots into two glasses. "A good chef always tastes his ingredients," he said, handing her one of the glasses, "Cheers!"

Now Colette, she told herself, taking a sip, *you're collecting the kids, so just one glass... but then... a little won't hurt.*

"How do you like your steak, Colette?"

"Oh, medium-rare," she replied, roused from her thoughts. "Thanks."

"Anything for you, darling."

In no time at all, the steak was dished up, along with fresh broccoli, roast potatoes and the Gaelic sauce. They sat at the table and began to eat.

Moseley seemed more relaxed now, and Colette started to wonder if she really wanted to end things yet. *Maybe I'll just sit back and enjoy one last evening of feeling pampered. I deserve it.* Moseley drew out the corkscrew from a bottle of red wine.

"Red or white wine?" he asked.

"I'd love some red, since you have it opened," Colette replied, in spite of herself.

"We are so alike," he said, pouring her a glass, "I bet you like banoffee pie too?"

"I do."

"Good, because that's what we're having for dessert."

"Thank you." She had begun to feel awkward again. The wine had reminded her of his behaviour the last time they had dinner. It wasn't a good memory.

"You deserve it," he said, reaching out to take her hand, but she quickly withdrew it, under the pretence of a small coughing fit.

"Are you alright?"

"Yeah," answered Colette. "I'm fine."

"So..." Moseley added, in a feeble attempt at starting a conversation, "How have you been?"

"Fine," she said, brushing his hand off lightly with an awkward laugh, "I wish you wouldn't treat me like an invalid, I'm practically better".

"Yes, you are improving rapidly, but you are not out of the woods yet."

When the main course was finished, Moseley placed a heaped

plate of banoffee pie in front of her. It was sprinkled with sugar. Colette was almost full, but she ate it anyway. She didn't want to hurt his feelings.

He was watching her closely. She wished he would stop and concentrate on his own food. His intense gaze was making her feel nervous.

"Do you like it?" he asked.

"It's delicious."

Colette began to feel very worn out. Moseley's behaviour was making her feel uncomfortable.

This is it, she thought, *I'll tell him now... I'm going to finish with him.*

Suddenly, she was exhausted. Her entire body felt much heavier than usual, and her head ached terribly.

That was sugar, wasn't it? Colette thought she saw a sly grin on Moseley's face before the blackness consumed her.

***

The Halloween party had been an unexpected success. It wasn't really a party, more of a slightly out-of-control festival for the whole school. Both Matt and Rachel had loved every bit of it, even the end, when someone stuck on a *One Direction* CD and everyone began to dance, pretending they were teeny boppers.

Colette had promised to come and pick them up for once. Matt and Rachel took this as a sign that she was getting better at long last. Even though they were almost the last to leave, they were sure she would come for them.

Matt licked his toffee apple as they waited on the footpath outside the school.

"Rachel," he said, feeling more relaxed and confident than he ever had before, "tonight, let's just pretend that there is nothing wrong with the world, that we're... normal".

She gave him a quizzical look, but it didn't put him off.

"Remember when we were little, we used to play imaginary games?"

Rachel chuckled softly. "Yeah and remember how Dad used to pick us both up and swing us around until he was red in the face from the effort?"

They smiled at each other for a second before Rachel put her two arms around Matt for the first time since either of them could remember and gave him a hug, almost smothering him.

"Hey, steady on," Matt protested, pulling away, "someone could be watching. I have a reputation to keep up here".

"You have a reputation? Matthew O'Connor, I am not even going to go there." She gave his hair a playful swipe, destroying his carefully coiffed peak with one motion of her fingers. "I shouldn't even be seen talking to you, you know," she laughed.

Several minutes went by.

"She's not coming, is she?" asked Matt, throwing his toffee apple stick over the school wall.

Having failed to reach Colette on her mobile twice, Rachel said, "Time to call my boyfriend, who couldn't even be bothered to show up tonight. Now he can pay by giving me a lift."

"What good is that to me? Can't we just walk?" Matt asked, as he watched his sister dial Derek's number.

"Well you're going to have to. My feet are really sore. Derek will come. He always does, especially when I lay the guilt stuff on him. You go on ahead, and we'll keep an eye on you, though you'll probably be home before the stupid twerp gets here."

"If you're sure. Will you be okay?"

Rachel reverted to her mafia voice to answer him: "Hello! Me okay? Yeah, now beat it punk if ya know what's good for ya."

Not wanting to spoil the mood, Matt did as his big sister told him. He knew that in spite of his tiredness, he would definitely be home before she was. Derek would surely take a detour.

Matt was right. He was home before Rachel. All the way back, he had kept an eye out for his mum. He had thought that Moseley calling around to cook dinner for her was an extremely bad idea. Nonetheless, she had promised that it would be a short affair, that she would use the occasion to finish it with him.

The sight of Colette's battered, old Ford Mondeo in the driveway confirmed that she had indeed forgotten them.

I shouldn't have let it happen. I should have made her listen to me. What if he treated her badly?

That and a million other thoughts raced through Matt's head as he opened the front door and went inside, calling out as he did so.

"Mum, are you home?"

Silence. *At least Moseley isn't here*, he thought. The idea of having to play the 'I'm-pretending-not-to-know-who-you-are,' game sickened him to his core. Yet he and Rachel had decided to play along, at least until they could extract Colette from the evil clutches of Moseley, and bring their dad back into their family. Then they would face everything together. He had told Rachel about Gabriel McNally's offer of help. Hopefully, he would be able to re-open the case, clear his father's name and restore them as a family. Matt longed for this.

I'd be careful if I were you, young Matthew.

Mr Freckles' warning sent a shiver through Matt as he tentatively trudged upstairs.

"Mum," he called again.

Through the partially opened bedroom door he could see Colette lying face down on her bed. She was dressed as she had been when he and Rachel had left for the Halloween party, but there was something unnatural about the way one of her arms was tucked in awkwardly under her.

"Mum!" Matt screamed, shaking Colette's shoulders. "Please Mum, wake up."

He looked around. On her bedside locker, there was a half empty bottle of gin, an empty pill box and a glass of water. Thoughts raced through his mind.

"Mum, wake up!"

Nothing. He turned her over into a more comfortable position and listened for a breath. After what seemed an eternity, he noticed a rattling sound. This was followed by a long silence before it came again, as if from deep down in her lungs.

Matt had learned about the recovery position in first aid class.

He tried to get his mother into it, but this was impossible on the soft bed. He tried to prop her up with pillows, but she rolled back onto her face. He was about to give up and call an ambulance when his mother took a sudden deep breath. Her stomach gave a massive heave. Colette's eyes flashed open. She brought two of her hands to her mouth and then extended an arm to Matt as if to ask for help. Matt half lifted, half dragged his mother to the en-suite bathroom where she vomited violently into the toilet.

"You're okay, Mum," said Matt, holding her hair away from her face. "You're all right now."

When she had finished throwing up, Matt helped her back to her bed. Ignoring her garbled apologies, he pulled back the bedclothes and got her to lie on her side. He removed her shoes and gently pulled the duvet over her. Happy that she had settled down, he fetched a large glass of water for her from the kitchen, along with some tissues and a basin in case she had to throw up again. As soon as she was comfortable and breathing regularly, Matt cleaned the bathroom. Then he began a vigil by his mother's bed.

After a while, he sent a text to Rachel asking her to come home. There was no response.

Twenty minutes later, Matt sent another text. Still, nothing came. He thought about texting David or maybe even Gabriel McNally, but he decided to wait until Rachel showed up. Making himself comfortable on the outside of Colette's bed, he positioned himself so that he could hear her breathing and just listened and waited. Despite the urgency and the worry that he felt, Matt found solace in his mother's steady breathing. He guessed that Moseley was at fault.

Maybe he had forced her to take tablets. Or had he slipped something into her food? Matt hoped that whatever it was, the vomiting had purged it from her system. He began to think of the first encrypted message that had come into David's phone. This must have been what Moseley was on about.

As he lay in the darkness, a plan began to unfold in Matt's mind. He would go to Agatha's. He would meet his dad. Together, and with the help of Gabriel McNally and the surveillance they now had on Moseley's phone, they would unveil this latest plot against his family. If only Rachel would come home.

The early morning sunlight was just making its way through the thick curtains when Colette awoke with a start. She tried to lift her head off the pillows but couldn't. The searing pain in her head made her feel as if her brain was swollen, trying to burst out of her skull. The pressure on the duvet told her that someone else was lying on her bed.

"Are you awake, Mum?"

The question was more of a whisper, filtering through the ache in her head and the glow of the growing morning light outside. It was Matt. Slowly the events of the previous night came back to her; her broken promise to collect her children, pretending to enjoy the dinner with Ricky, slipping down into a fog of oblivion, and emerging briefly into consciousness to find herself throwing up in the bathroom. Her last memory, of Matt's helping hand keeping her head out of the toilet, was the worst of all.

"You shouldn't have to see that, Mattie." She turned and put her arms around her son.

"It's all right, Mum. Don't worry about it."

"Things will be different now. You'll never have to see anything like that, ever again."

"Would you like some water?" he asked, a little awkward at his mother's apology.

"Yes, please."

He let her drink before breaking the news to her, "Rachel didn't come home last night."

"Are you sure?" Colette asked, trying to sit up. "Maybe she came in when we were sleeping."

"I didn't sleep. I was too worried about you and Rachel. I just listened, and she didn't come in."

Matt relayed the events of the previous night, from his parting with his sister to where they were now.

"What time is it?" Colette asked, dragging her legs over the side of the bed.

"Just past six. I sent her a load of text messages, but she didn't reply to any of them. If I had Derek's number, I'd call him, but I don't."

Colette was slow to react. She groaned and leaned back on her pillows before going into the bathroom. When he heard the retching again, Matt went to help her, but his mother stretched out a hand to stop him. He backed off and went downstairs.

Matt and Colette waited until half past seven and then began to call around Rachel's friends. No one could help them, so they decided to take the car and drive around, retracing possible journeys from the school to Derek's house. Derek's parents were sympathetic, bringing them in for tea. When Derek came sleepily downstairs, it soon became clear that he hadn't met Rachel after all. They had argued on the phone, and Rachel had decided to walk home by herself. At this point everyone became very worried.

Colette and Matt drove to the police station. They stood at the high counter, but it was a good five minutes before a Garda appeared from a back room. He seemed reluctant to leave the comfort of his office.

"My daughter is missing," Colette said.

"Since when?" said the police officer. The name Frank Kelly was on his name tag. He pulled a form from somewhere underneath the counter and clicked a pen.

"She didn't come home last night after the school disco. I've tried all her friends. No one has heard anything from her."

"That's not long, ma'am. I'm sure there is a good explanation. What age is your daughter?"

"Fifteen. She had never done this before. You have to help us. Please."

Colette was desperate. It made Matt angry to hear the plaintive note in her voice.

The man called a female police officer from the room behind. Straight away, Matt and Colette recognised the young Garda who had visited their home when Rachel had been caught shoplifting.

"These people are reporting a missing teenager," the male officer explained to his colleague. She looked sympathetically at them as he relayed the situation.

"Mrs O'Connor isn't it?" the female Garda asked.

"Yes."

"Your daughter isn't officially a missing person and won't be for 48 hours. She could be home before you get back.

"Aren't you going to help us? Colette was angry now. Matt was surprised at her sudden change.

"You need to stay calm Mrs O'Connor. Certainly we can do a run around in the general area, but she's probably with friends or maybe at a house party," said Kelly. This angered Colette even more. Her speech was slightly slurred when she answered.

"You have always been against us. You never believed that my husband was innocent. You stopped looking for him before. Now you are refusing to help me again."

Matt was puzzled by the aggression in her voice. He knew it wouldn't help. The female officer took up the challenge.

"Did you drive here this morning, Mrs O'Connor?"

"What do you mean?" Colette was very agitated.

"Were you drinking last night? Maybe you shouldn't be driving if you are upset. My colleague and I can leave you back, and I'm sure your daughter will make her way home in no time."

Colette was even more upset now and Matt tried to intervene. "Come on, Mum. Let's do what they say."

"No, I won't come on, Matt. This is just the way I remember it. Let's go!"

Colette stormed out of the Garda station with Matt trailing behind her.

When they got into the car, Colette started it and took off quickly, almost too quickly. Her driving was erratic, jerky.

After two minutes, Matt looked out the window and everything was just a blur.

"Eh, Mum, are you sure you're not going over the speed limit?"

"Don't worry Matt," she took her eyes off the road and looked at him, "because according to the Guards, it doesn't matter. They're too lazy to chase after me".

"MUM WATCH OUT!" screamed Matt.

Colette slammed on the brakes, but it was too late. They had crashed into a brand new Skoda. Colette's head snapped forward and banged against the steering wheel. In less than five minutes, an ambulance and the Guards were on the scene. Matt heard their voices as he sat in a daze caused by shock and lack of sleep.

"It's her again," said a familiar female voice. "Frank, tell the paramedics we'll need two stretchers."

Disaster, Matt thought, as they were lifted into the ambulance. *Rachel is missing, Mum's out of her mind, and Moseley is breathing down my neck. Things are about as bad as they can get.*

***

Matt was sitting beside his mother's hospital bed when a doctor walked in.

"Hello Matt."

Matt glanced at him and quickly looked away before answering. "Hi."

"You only have a few minor cuts and bruises, but your mother has suffered from whiplash and will need a little rest. We'll keep her here for a few hours, but you are free to go home. Is there someone you can call to pick you up?"

"My aunty is on her way," Matt lied.

"I'll leave you to it, then," the doctor said.

Once the doctor had gone, Matt went to the payphone at the end of the ward and called David.

"Hello?"

"David!" exclaimed Matt. "Right, listen. Rachel has gone missing, and Mum and I were in a car crash this morning. You have to get me out of here."

Twenty minutes later, Matt was waiting at the hospital door for David and his mother. When they arrived in their car, he asked them to drive him to Agatha's house. He needed help.

*****

This is not happening, Rachel told herself, *I am at home, in bed, having a nightmare.* She sighed. No matter how much she pretended, she couldn't disguise the fact that blood was dripping down her face. She was bound and gagged, and from the excruciating pain she felt, she probably had a broken finger. Rachel strained her ears for any sound or clue that could help her. From the front of the van, she could hear snippets of her captors' conversation.

"Moseley, we should have got the two of them. You're still making contact with the boy?" The voice was low... gruff.

"Yes boss." The voice that answered was vaguely familiar.

Who is it? Wait... Rachel gritted her teeth to stop herself screaming every foul word she knew. It was Ricky Moseley! *I knew we shouldn't have trusted him.*

A small voice in the back of Rachel's mind said, *your mother loves him.*

"Shut up!" Rachel said aloud. Then, she was quiet again, listening intently.

Moseley's boss was speaking. "Yes, but you should have encouraged him to stay home. Then we could have got both of them."

Ha! Serves you right! Rachel thought. Then she stiffened. Someone had mentioned her father.

"If we had taken all three of them, there would be no one to raise the alarm, and O'Connor might never hear about it."

"You're sure they're not in touch with him?"

"No, idiot. If a missing person turned up, it would be in the papers."

"Oh yeah... "

A silence fell on the group, giving Rachel unwanted time to dwell on her situation. *I'm gonna die! Standing there waiting for that stupid Derek to come and get me and these thugs come out of nowhere. I should have fought harder. Shouldn't have let them take me.* Questions raced through her confused mind as she tried to make some sense, any sense of her situation.

Arrghh! The van had taken a sharp turn, toppling Rachel, who was bound so tightly that she had no control over any of her limbs, banging her head against the metal side.

"Owwww... " she groaned, as her bare legs scraped against the floor of the van. *Why did I have to be kidnapped after a party?* Now she lay on her back, where she had fallen, and went through her ever-growing list of injuries. *This sucks*, she thought, before passing out again.

She was awoken sometime later by the van stopping abruptly. She lay in the dark. The ropes were cutting into her, and she could barely feel her feet. The rough canvas that had been thrown over her when she was shoved into the van was severely limiting her oxygen intake, and she was feeling light-headed. Voices could be heard from outside. They seemed to be coming closer. Then, the door opened, exposing Rachel to a sharp biting wind. As hands roughly lifted her onto the gravel, she wobbled, as her numb feet tried to find purchase on the slippery ground.

"Walk!" Moseley grunted, cutting the tape that had bound her ankles. This was no easy task for Rachel, but she had no choice.

They were in a small car park that was empty apart from Moseley's van. Great big rows of barbed wire separated Rachel from the world.

"Let me go, you..." she screamed, but it only came out as a murmur from beneath the fat, smelly hand that covered her mouth. She wriggled around, trying to escape, but to no avail.

Rachel was led to a concealed door on the right of the building. Moseley's accomplice entered a code into a small keypad beside it. He pushed the door open, revealing a long corridor filled with filing cabinets and assorted building materials. They trudged to the end and took a right. Then they entered a small room with grey walls and little furniture apart from a bare table and wooden chair in the corner. They thrust Rachel into the chair and quickly tied two skipping ropes around her chest and legs, pinning her tightly to the chair back. Amid the terribleness of her situation, Rachel found time to wonder where Moseley had found the children's skipping ropes he used to tie her up.

"Can you feel your legs?" Moseley asked, faking concern

"Yes, thank you," Rachel answered sarcastically.

"Let me fix that for you," he said, tightening the ropes.

"Too tight, I can't breathe," she pleaded.

"Shut up. You are staying here until I get what I want!" Ricky approached Rachel before speaking again. "Where is your father?"

"Are you crazy? I don't know!" Rachel was gasping for breath. Ricky knelt down and put his face close to Rachel's.

"I am going to ask you once more only. Where's your father?"

Rachel spat in his face. Lashing out with her two legs, she tried to kick Moseley, but he laughed and blocked her easily.

"Nice try."

Think Rachel, think.

"Fine," she said eventually, sobbing, "I'll tell you."

Moseley grabbed her by the shoulders and pressed his face up to hers, flecks of his spit spraying her as he said excitedly; "Well? Where is he?"

"He... he's in Portlaoise... hiding."

"Portlaoise is huge. Where?"

"He moves around."

"I'm going to make this clear, you are only bait. But if you don't co-operate, I can get someone else. You are disposable. Got that?"

This statement was accompanied by a hard slap to Rachel's face, causing her to cry out in pain. She held back the tears, determined not to cry in front of her captors.

"Yeah."

"So unless you want to be disposed of, you'd better give me some details."

"Uh... I..."

Just then, Moseley's phone beeped. He looked at his message.

"Very sorry," he said with an evil grin. "I'll have to get back to you, but just in case you get any bright ideas... I'll leave you my friend."

He disappeared for a moment and then returned with a massive Rottweiler, growling with his hackles raised. Moseley looped his lead around a small pole in the corner, "He will keep you company," he sneered.

With Moseley gone, Rachel knew that this was her one and only chance to escape.

"*Think Rachel, think... Eureka!*"

Carefully Rachel managed to get to her feet, keeping a wary eye on the dog. Judging by what she could see of his lead, he could only go a few metres in any direction, but she would have to get past him if she were to get to the door. He became highly agitated when she moved. She braced herself, *1, 2, and 3!* She ran backwards as fast as she could, slamming against the rough concrete wall. The chair broke instantly.

"Yes!"

Massaging her aching head, Rachel felt the ropes loosen about her. With some jerks and twists she freed herself and brushed off the splinters.

"Now for the dog," she muttered.

"I could free the dog easily enough, but he would go for me straight away... FOOD!"

On a table in the other side of the room were the remains of a snack that Moseley had been eating earlier... a half-eaten bag of crisps and a few sticks of gum. Putting a few pieces of gum into her mouth and giving it a quick chew, Rachel began to formulate her plan.

I guess it's worth a try.

Summoning up more courage than she'd ever needed in her fifteen years, she approached the straining animal with the titbits. Sure enough, the dog ambled towards the food. While keeping an occasional eye on Rachel, it greedily snaffled up the crisps in one gulp.

Uh-Oh.

Rachel hadn't counted on it eating so fast. When the dog had gulped up the large ball of gum, Rachel decided that it was now or never. She made a run for the door. The Rottweiler pounced at her and bit her leg, causing excruciating pain, but she kept running.

The dog chased her but then suddenly stopped. It made a strange sound and then started pawing at its throat. Rachel didn't hesitate, she bolted for the door.

Gum must be stuck in his throat.

***

Agatha picked up the phone.

"Hello?" she said.

"Agatha, I don't mean to interrupt but... you didn't dial the number yet," Matt reminded her.

"Oh dearie me. I only got this phone last year, and I haven't got the hang of it yet." She began to dial Ronan's number.

"It's fine."

Okay, Matt thought, *I'm going to talk to my Dad for the first time in seven years.*

A series of questions raced through his mind.

What will I say to him? What will he think of me?

After what seemed like ages, Agatha got through.

"Hello, hello? Yes, it's Agatha. I'm fine, thanks."

Matt froze. He heard a low voice coming from the other end of the phone.

"Matt, someone wants to talk to you."

Matt took a deep breath. *Okay I'm ready.* Agatha handed him the phone, but he held it at a distance.

I'm not ready, I'm not ready.

"Come on dearie. He's waiting to talk to you."

Okay here goes. Matt put the receiver to his ear.

"Hello?" Matt barely whispered.

"Matthew, it it... it's you."

"Y...y... yes," Matt closed his eyes, but this didn't hold back the tears that welled up.

"Matthew, there is no need to be frightened. It's only me, your father."

"I miss you," Matt blurted out.

"I know you do, and I miss you too, so much."

"Then why don't you come home?"

"Matthew... "

"It's Matt."

"Okay, Matt. It's not that easy. According to the police, I'm one of the worst criminals in Ireland."

"Well if you can't come home, tell me where you are so I can come and see you, please?" Matt pleaded through the tears.

"I'm here son, turn around."

Matt turned around. There standing in the doorway was a middle-aged man, with brown hair like Matt's and the same blue eyes as Rachel. Matt dropped the phone. He stood there in disbelief.

After a long silence, Agatha said, "Would you like a cup of tea?"

They sat down.

"Dad," Matt said shakily. He could feel tears streaming down his face.

"You left us, why? Seven years and you only show your face now when Mum is trying to forget about you." Matt could feel his courage building up. Now it was more anger than fear.

"Matt, I can... "

"Seven years we waited, Dad. You left us to go poor, for Rachel to steal, for Mum to take medication when she didn't need it."

"Rachel did what?"

"She stole, because of you. Now, she's gone missing. Well, since last night anyway. Mum and I went looking for her, and Mum was so upset that she drove too fast and crashed. They took us to the hospital. She's still there."

Everything went quiet. Ronan stared at his son in disbelief.

"Tea time," Agatha announced, her timing perfect. She landed a biscuit tin in the centre of the table and poured tea into three china mugs. They sipped in silence.

Ronan eventually managed to speak. "Is your mother alright?"

"Yeah. She's okay. It's just whiplash. She'll be out later on."

"And what do you think has happened to Rachel?"

"Well, she's not at Derek's house. He's her boyfriend. But she has lots of friends from her swimming club, and I heard her planning something with a girl called Sandy a while back. I tried to tell Mum this, but she wouldn't listen... just went off her rocker and dragged us down to the Garda station."

I'm really sorry, Matt. I'll help you find her, but first I think I owe you an explanation."

Matt looked expectantly at his father.

"Before I start talking, tell me, should I be worried about your sister? Tell me truthfully now."

"No. She'll call or come home soon enough," Matt said, a little too confidently. His desire to speak with his dad was outweighing any other concerns.

"If you're absolutely sure." Seeing his son nod, Ronan O'Connor continued, "You have to understand that if I had stayed, I would be in prison! I did it all for you, Colette and Rachel. I had no choice. And I am so, so sorry."

"I'm sorry too."

Agatha opened the tin of biscuits and gave them a shake.

"Who's for a custard cream?" she asked. Ronan reached over and took out two. He handed one to Matt.

"Thanks," Matt muttered. "Dad, how did you manage to disappear without a trace?"

"Well," began Ronan, "it really is a rather long story."

"I've waited for seven years. I think I have the time now."

"First, we are going to have to call your mother, maybe get her over here," said Ronan. He looked meaningfully at Agatha, and she smiled.

"I'll call her while you two boys have a good old catch up. She's at the hospital, you say? And I'll see if there is any news on poor Rachel while I'm at it."

"Thanks Agatha, I would appreciate that very much."

"And I think I should call Gabriel McNally too by the sound of it? I think we really need him, and he will be over in a jiffy."

Ronan nodded his approval before turning once again to his son.

"Okay then son, I think you're old enough now to be told what really happened. As you know already, it began the day of the fire, which was started by a gang of men who would have done anything to get their hands on the Irish Crown Jewels. We had a not-so-little gun battle, in the woods. Two of them followed me into the cover.

They were shooting. I was running, trying to lure them away, so that your mother could get you and Rachel to safety. One of the men, I shot; the one who eventually did the stretch in jail. The other one was helping him, bringing him back to safety. I didn't want that so I shouted back at him and held up the case that contained the jewels. This worked; he came after me. Eventually, I doubled back. He was becoming entangled in the thickets, distracted, and I waited for him. I waited, and then I killed him."

Ronan's voice had become little more than a whisper. For a moment, he buried his face in his hands as if trying to stop himself from seeing what was in his mind.

"By this time," he said eventually, "I could hear the police sirens. I knew that the raid had been a failure. But, Matt, I panicked and did something... something horrible... something I'll see for the rest of my life, every night when I close my eyes. If I could turn back the clock and do things differently, I would, but that can't be done. I decided to swap my ring for his, my coat for his, my watch and my shoes. All before setting fire to him. Everyone believed me to be dead. I'm not a murderer Matt, you have to believe it. I did it to protect my family." He looked at Matt, his eyes begging for some sign of forgiveness.

Matt's tears had dried on his cheeks. He felt the anger begin to bubble inside him again, but he didn't know what to say.

"Anyone for another biscuit?" said Agatha, in an awkward attempt to break the silence. When neither of them answered, she put the tin back on the table and topped up their cups of tea before sitting back in her chair in respectful silence.

Ronan took a deep breath and continued with his story. "I took whatever money I needed from the safe and made my way to Dublin. I hid in a van so that I could get onto a ferry and travel to England without having my passport."

"Did it work?"

"Oh it did," said Ronan, "It worked perfectly. When I arrived in England I got a train to Manchester. I stayed there with my very trustworthy first cousin, Dan, until I got a forged passport made. Then I left Britain and flew to America. Once I arrived in New York, I got a train to Boston where I opened a bank account and withdrew a small amount of money. I also rented a flat for a while. Then I moved on to Chicago. I did the exact same there. I spent about a month safely in Chicago and then I went on to Louisiana, and on to Vegas soon after that. When I was sure I wasn't being trailed, I went back to the airport. I got the plane back to Ireland. I knew I had to go back, to keep an eye on you and Rachel. You think I missed out on your whole life, but I didn't, you just didn't know. There was money which I transferred to your mother's account and recently, when things went downhill, I left food parcels."

"I knew it," said Matt. "I don't know how, but somehow, I knew you were there." He reached over and put his hand on his father's shoulder, the sign of forgiveness Ronan was looking for.

"Thanks, son."

Agatha interrupted them to say that a taxi had just pulled up outside. It was Colette.

"Are you sure you're ready to meet her?" Matt asked Ronan.

"As ready as I'll ever be," his father answered with a nervous grin.

"Oh sorry dear, they are in the kitchen having some refreshments. I have the kettle on," they heard Agatha explain to Colette.

The door opened.

"Colette!" Ronan exclaimed. Colette walked towards him and... smack! She slapped him right across the face.

Ronan raised a hand to his cheek and groaned.

"That's what you get for leaving us here to rot! All to protect your stupid jewels! We thought you were dead!" Ronan lifted his hand off his cheek, which was as red as a tomato.

"Oh... I'm sorry," said Colette and slapped him again.

"Okay, okay," spluttered Ronan, raising his hands in supplication. "But Colette, you know what a big responsibility I had. I had to protect Ireland's most valuable jewels and to do that, I couldn't get caught! I had a lawless gang on my trail and once they'd eliminated me, they would have disposed of you too."

Colette sucked in a deep breath and slowly let it out.

"I should be glad you're alive, but I'm not. I only came here because your daughter has gone missing, and you just might want to know where she's gone, because nobody else seems to care."

At this point, Agatha bustled over with a fresh pot of tea and an extra cup.

"More tea!" she announced.

"I've had enough," replied Ronan, "but I do need something for my face". He smiled weakly at Colette, in an effort to show that there were no hard feelings.

The doorbell rang. This time it was Gabriel McNally. He seemed strangely calm when he saw Ronan sitting at the kitchen table. The old man introduced himself, pulled up a chair, and accepted the cup of tea that was quickly offered.

Relieved that the sparks had stopped flying, Matt told his parents everything, explaining the seriousness of the situation he and David had uncovered. A shocked Colette tried hard to scold him when she heard about all the times he had mitched from school, but she retreated into a stunned silence when Matt told them about his online friendship with Noname101 and how he had turned out to be Ricky Moseley. Matt finished by describing the technological hub he had set up in Agatha's sitting room and the plan he and Gabriel had devised to contact the police.

Gabriel smiled wryly at Ronan. "You know who this Ricky Moseley character is, of course?"

"No," began Ronan, looking confused, but then it hit him. "He's one of them, isn't he?"

"Ricky Molloy," said Gabriel. "I'm fairly sure he's never forgiven you for shooting him and landing him a six year stretch in prison."

Ronan looked angrily at Colette. "You let him into our house!"

Indignation overcoming her shock, Colette retaliated, "How was I to know who he was? And if you had been with us, like you should have been..."

"No wonder Rachel's gone missing!" Ronan countered.

"Easy now. This is no time for recriminations." In a calm but firm voice, Gabriel restored peace. "You say your daughter is missing?" he asked Colette.

When Colette explained, Gabriel's face became very serious. He took out his phone and made several calls to people he knew in the police force. Within a few short minutes, the Guards had agreed to upgrade Rachel's disappearance to one of "missing," and they seemed to respond seriously when Gabriel outlined the danger the O'Connor family faced.

Finally, Gabriel put the phone down.

"This is it, Ronan," he said. "I may be wrong, but I'm fairly sure there's a link between your daughter's disappearance and the efforts of Ricky Molloy aka Moseley to ingratiate himself into your family. We have to get your daughter back and put this gang out of business once and for all. Now you folks will have to grab what you can and get yourselves back here as quickly as possible. We will also need Matt's young friend to help with the IT side of things. The police are picking him up and meeting you back at Forest View. They'll be discreet, but you'll all have to hurry."

Less than thirty minutes later, Matt was grabbing what he could from his room. Mr Freckles, who had spent the last twenty-four hours in Matt's wardrobe, seemed oblivious to the gravity of the situation.

Ah! Young Matthew. I thought you would never return. I hope you have come to put right the previous fault of abandoning me in this miniscule sleeping chamber and the delights that it does not contain.

Matt screwed up his face in confusion, "If that means you were lonely... "

Lonely? Moi? Not in the slightest! How dare you!"

"Really? News flash. We are going to stay with Agatha, in the surveillance hub, all of us so... Bye!"

Wait! Mr Freckle's voice echoed within his head. Matt smiled to himself as he turned back to his wooden friend. "Yes? What was that?"

I wish to accompany you on this escapade to the residence of Miss Agatha and, how did you put it, 'check-up' on this 'surveillance hub.' I should like to provide you with the pleasure of my company as you travel to Miss Agatha's.

"What? All right then. You can come, but no funny business."

Funny business. Why, Matthew, funny business is my middle name, and you know what we say... no matter what, the show must go on.

- 21 -

FRECKLES GOES WI-FI

Matt sat on the wall in front of his house, drinking from a bottle of Fanta. He was watching his parents pack his life away into cardboard boxes and place them in the van. They were leaving the furniture behind – it would be too bulky for Agatha's house and there just wasn't room in the van. Matt smiled to see his parents together again once more. After their earlier argument, they were being very civil to each other.

David, who had been delivered in an unmarked police car, nudged him the ribs, "Earth to Matt, Earth to Matt. Come in, Matt?"

Matt didn't move. His face was blank, his eyes staring into space. He was deep in thought. David rolled his eyes and knocked gently on the side of Matt's skull, "Helloo-o, is anyone home?" He clicked his fingers in front of his friend's nose.

Matt was startled out of his reverie. The first words out of his mouth were, "I didn't do it."

"What?" David asked. "No, no. I was telling a joke. That is, before you switched to 'off mode.'"

"Sorry. I was thinking. Tell it again."

"Okay, what is Santa's favourite drink in the summer?"

"Umm..."

"You're supposed to say, 'I don't know,'" David whispered helpfully.

"Oh, okay. I don't know."

"Fanta Claus!"

"Seriously?"

"What?"

"That was one of the worst jokes I have ever heard."

"It wasn't that bad."

"It was terrible. Call yourself Professor Messer?"

"I am so..."

"Then find better jokes."

"Oh fine, what's..."

"Heard it."

"You don't even know what I was going to say!"

"You were going to say what's black, white, red and sometimes boring? Duh, a newspaper. I can see it in your eyes."

"Then why... "

"Next, please."

"Okay. Who's going to get squished?"

"That's not even a joke."

"It will be once I get to the *punch* line!"

David gave Matt a friendly punch and fell about laughing. Matt looked at him wearily.

"I never noticed it before, but you really have bad taste in jokes."

"I do not."

Ronan stuck his head out of the van window. "Are you two coming or are you just going to sit there arguing for the rest of your lives? Get in the back."

The boys climbed into the back of the van, closed the door and settled in among the boxes as it pulled off.

Mr Freckles insisted on complaining all the way to Agatha's house, or as he put it, 'the lady's residence.'

Look, Freckles, I don't know why I'm bringing you, Matt groaned inside his head. *All you seem to do is drive me nuts! You're good at it too.*

Ah, you have not yet set eyes upon the full extent of the ingenuity of my curiously wonderful magic!

Wow. Just wow. What do you want, a show? A cloak? A wand? You've already got a top hat.

Most amusing.

All magic tricks are 'amusing.'

As usual Matthew, your sense of humour never ceases to amaze me. You are even beginning to sound a little like me, and that has to be a positive development.

Like yours, my mouth is one big magic trick.

Soon, the van came to a stop at Agatha's. She was standing in the porch. Matt jumped out of the van, Mr Freckles in tow.

Hello, Mistress Agatha! Mr Freckles yelled. *How are you this fine afternoon?*

Matt felt a new presence in his mind for the first time.

Tickles? How good it is to hear your voice in my head again.

Matt gasped. "Agatha? You can hear it too?"

The old woman smiled. "Yes. Your great grandfather taught me how to do it when I was a little girl living here."

You were a fine beauty then, Mr Freckles said. *That certainly hasn't changed.*

Agatha gave a girlish giggle. "Oh, stop it, Tickles."

"Uh, why do you call him Tickles?" Matt enquired.

"That's what he used to be called. Tickles, the amazing talking dummy!"

"Well he's Freckles now."

That's Mr Freckles to you, you young scallywag!

"Come on, Matt," called Ronan, "give us a hand here".

Agatha realised that they were still standing outside. "Oh goodness gracious me, we'll catch our death of cold! Come in, come in. I'll make some camomile tea."

As the O'Connor family's possessions were transferred to the house, Mr Freckles continued to natter. *So, mistress, how are you doing with the surreality pub?*

"Surveillance hub..." Matt groaned, slapping his own forehead. "It's a surveillance hub you dummy!"

More cars could be heard pulling into the driveway. Matt stuffed Mr Freckles into his backpack and went to help unpack. In the space of two hours, the house of Agatha Fox was crawling with more technology, police men and women, and personnel than it was capable of holding. They were in almost every room, out on the front lawn, and in every nook and cranny.

Ronan, Colette, Gabriel McNally and several Guards stood behind Matt and David as they sat at the computer and switched it on.

"You know, this place is like our hub," whispered Matt.

"Yeah, like mission control."

Matt typed in the password. It didn't work.

"Agatha," he shouted. "What have you done to my password?"

"It's Frolicking in Flowers," Agatha shouted from the kitchen.

Several of the Guards laughed. Matt went red with embarrassment and typed in the password. Then David took over. He opened the relevant file and input Matt's phone password.

Hello? Get me out of this napping satchel, I can help! Mr Freckles insisted.

No offence, Matt said as lightly as possible, *but I don't think you can do much right now.*

I have mastered the inner peecee!

"Really?" Matt asked in disbelief. To everyone's surprise, he lifted Mr Freckles out of the bag and put him on the table beside the computer.

I'll show you! Freckles focused his inner energy on creating a virtual shell of himself within the machine, leaving his present wooden shell in the real world. The reality for those who were looking at him was the image of a frozen Freckles, sitting upright looking even more rigid and wooden than ever, if that were possible. Matt began to worry about him. The dummy had apparently left the room and moved into the virtual world of the information super highway. Although Matt didn't know it yet, Mr Freckles was having the virtual time of his life as he witnessed the millions of floating pixels and software applications and instructions flying either side of him. Emails and text documents flew everywhere like flies. As he moved he noticed his walking was not as smooth as reality. Freckles was locked up in the frame rate of the PC. Below him, there was something that seemed to be a green hologram floor, almost liquid in form, which contained a plasma-like river of images. Mr Freckles gazed in wondrous awe at the endless stream of video clips, data, messages, tweets, apps, emails, gmails, movie scenes, sound bites, advertisements for everything under the sun. Above him, there was nothing but oblivion. Freckles' virtual shell began to fly around at his command, unable to focus on any of the confusion below him.

He... hello... Matt?

"Where are you, Freckles?"

I'm in the peecee's Wi-Fi... I think?

"Holy cow!" Matt said in surprise.

A strange, crackling noise came from the PC, and suddenly Mr Freckles' voice emerged from its speakers.

"I'm travelling into some kind of a web, a network. Hopefully, I will be able to find Moseley's phone." Mr Freckles' voice had an echo, as if he was talking over a long distance phone line.

"Try to find something called Meteor," Matt urged, ignoring the gasps of surprise that were coming from behind him.

Mr Freckles began to virtually whiz around, leaving a trail of green pixels behind him. Soaring around until he saw what Matt was talking about, Mr Freckles was soon buzzing around in the Meteor world where millions of phone messages and texts were floating past. Focusing on the name Ricky Moseley, he soon found the last location of the number, seeing five bars building up, each one higher than the last, all of them green. *I believe they show that our signal is a good one,* Freckles thought to himself. Then the names in the data confirmed that he had the correct phone. *Aha!* he thought. He switched into turbo drive, speeding into the bars. All of a sudden he could see out of the screen of Moseley's phone. Immediately, he heard a voice yelling, 'She's escaped, boss. The dog was watching her and she must have got past him.' It had an echo as if in an empty building, a warehouse.

"I can hear Moseley talking," said Mr Freckles. "Now, I can see him. He is talking about your sister, I think. It appears that she has eluded her captors."

"That's where she is!" Matt replied. "Have you anything more?" he said to Freckles. "Can you see Rachel?"

The Guards in the room, along with Colette and Ronan, were all looking incredulous. Gabriel McNally quelled the growing disillusion.

"Don't knock it folks. In my years in the force I've seen everything, from shrinks to psychics to witchdoctors, used to solve crimes. Besides, just take one look at poor Mr Freckles there. It has to be obvious to even the most cynical of you that the lights may be on, but there's no one home." He knocked three times on the wooden head, as if to emphasise his point. "Well on second thoughts, maybe the lights aren't on after all, but he is definitely zooming about out there somewhere, and it's him that's talking, believe me."

"He has just exited a warehouse," said Freckles, "most vexed... pointing towards a building named Centre, no Centra. He is driving around... scouring the area. A lot of people... purchases in bags... I can now see a golden island. It has a dome, I think. Now, he is going in the opposite direction. I see twin towers."

"You mean the Athlone cathedral?"

"I'm in an urban area... driving towards a great angry river... yes twin towers and a green dome."

"Athlone?" Matt asked.

"No need for name calling!"

"No, are you in Athlone?"

"No Matthew, I already told you I'm in a phone! Not what you call Athlone, but now I can see a, oh yes, a 'Welcome to Athlone' sign so... yes, I do know where I am. I am in Athlone. And I do recall the great Count, John Mc Cormac. Ah, what a most wondrous voice. Did I ever tell you about the time...?"

"Freckles! We know you are in Athlone. Now please concentrate and find my sister. You do know that we can now hear everything you are saying as actual sound."

"What, as speech? Human speech?"

"Yes."

"This is wondrous, magnificent. Who is present, Mathew, that I may address the assembly in proper fashion. You do not know how long I have waited, nay, dreamed of... "

"Freckles, try to focus."

"My lords and ladies, Mistress Agatha and members of the Royal

Irish Constabulary, it is with great humility... no, not humility, but a pleasure indeed to place in your service the persona of one Mr Freckles Shackleton, ah none other than my good..."

"Freckles, please shut up and tell us what you see. Can you see my sister anywhere?"

"If you do insist so," Freckles said sarcastically. "I can see someone running in the distance and yes, it does look like... argh!"

"Mr Freckles, what's happening? Talk to me!"

The group fell silent, waiting for some clue. Colette was the first to react. "Where is she, Mr Freckles? Please tell us something."

No message came.

"For God's sake," Gabriel roared at his former colleagues, "Do I have to drive to Athlone myself or are you going to rescue this little girl?" He was livid now, his nose becoming an even deeper shade of purple than normal.

The sudden explosion of emotion from the normally jolly man brought an immediate response from the officer in command, Superintendent Finlay.

He picked up his walkie talkie. "All units. Focus on the Golden Island area of Athlone. A missing girl, name, Rachel O'Connor, most likely on foot, last seen heading for the river, south of the shopping centre and may be in danger. We believe she is being pursued by a man in a blue Ford Transit van. This man is Ricky Molloy, a known criminal. Extreme caution is to be exercised. Subject may be armed. Repeat, subject may be armed." The officer moved out into the hallway.

Colette took Matt in her arms. Cautiously, Ronan joined them, encircling them both. For the first time in seven years, Colette allowed herself to be touched by her husband. She broke down, as the possibility of losing her daughter loomed before her. This realisation caused her to recoil from Ronan's grasp as if the memory of whose fault this was came back to her. She bent down, leaning on Matt in her misery.

Agatha intervened. "Here dear, sit yourself down beside the fire. I have fresh tea made, and some nice scones. The right people are in charge now. Everything will work out, just you wait and see."

"Thanks, Agatha," Colette managed, as she sipped the comforting brew.

The tension of the moment was further interrupted by the sudden sound of Mr Freckles falling off his perch on a chair. Matt immediately ran to restore him to his seated position. "You're back!"

He had exited the Wi-Fi, immediately feeling all of the physical world come back to him, getting used to his wooden body again. *Curses, for once in my life I was free!*

"You're a hero!" said Matt. "Can you tell us anything else about Rachel?"

I am sorry, Matthew. It seems that the felon may have dropped his telephone. My last memory is of a fast-approaching surface coming up to meet me. You are familiar with the old Irish phrase, 'may the road rise to meet you?' That, my young friend best sums up my final experience of that wild and wonderful world of the internal network.

- 22 -

ESCAPE

The chaos of sounds in the intelligence hub came to a sudden stop when Colette's phone rang.

"Five rings," the Garda superintendent shouted, "5, 4, 3, 2 and 1, and answer!"

Ronan answered, "Hello?"

"Hello, Ronan, how're the kids? Oh wait, I have one of them. You should be asking me that," the voice said.

"Keep him on the line," Finlay mouthed.

"Who's there with you, Ronan? The lovely Colette? Is she missing me?"

"Be quiet," Finlay hissed to everyone. "Are we tracking?" he asked the operator.

"Tracking and recording, the feed is good," the reply came.

"What more do you want from me and my family?"

"It's simple, Rachel for the jewels."

"How do I know you actually have her?"

Moseley played a recording of Rachel's voice.

"You harm one hair on my daughter's head, and I'll finish the job I started on you seven years ago, do you hear me?" Ronan snarled.

"Ronan, Ronan, my man, don't worry yourself. She's loving it here. Let's just arrange our little trade, and we can all move on. What do you say?"

"Sure. Where and when?"

"I'll give you the details later, but if anyone but you shows up there, Ronan, the girl gets it. Do you know where I'm coming from? An eye for an eye?"

"Yeah, I understand."

"Besides, you already owe us."

The line went dead.

"Drat. Well, it's coming from some place in Athlone, East of the Shannon, just near the water tower mast," the Garda intelligence officer said.

"Right," Finlay barked, "get units down there. Comb the bloody place. Seal it off."

***

The warehouse stood hunched over the Shannon, like an old man who was just about ready to keel over and die. A man, Trent, walked along a pavement leading up to the warehouse, as casually as any escaped convict pretending to be an innocent citizen knows how.

He spoke quietly into his mobile phone, "No sign of any cops, boss. Looks like Moseley hasn't screwed this one up... yet".

A muffled response, "Yeah, I know, but really how hard can it be to hold a little girl captive?"

Just then a tall girl with long blonde hair burst through the warehouse door and pushed through the busy shoppers. She knocked against a canvas bag, and a carton of milk fell to the ground and burst open.

Trent stood for a moment with his mouth hanging open then said into the phone, "Call you back, Boss."

Snapping the phone shut, he started to run after the girl. Suddenly, another man stepped in front of him.

"Who do you think you are, chasing after a defenceless little girl?" Then, to the girl, the man yelled, "Run! I'll call the police!"

Rachel dared to glance behind for an instant, glad to catch sight of the melee that might just give her a chance. She ran with the hill, down and towards the river, unsure where the narrow little road would lead her. At least it was away from Moseley and the other man.

Trent growled in frustration and swiped viciously at the two men who had dared to block him before making good his escape, leaving both men shocked and bloody. He started after Rachel.

Rachel limped down the bleak alleyway, the pain in her leg excruciating. The cold cut through her thin clothes. But for all her discomfort, she knew she had just one chance to save her own life, and this was it.

If only I can get to a phone.

She was at the edge of the river now.

I must find people. Golden Island! I know where I am.

Then she saw the van.

Moseley... have to get past him... have to get help.

So far Moseley hadn't seen her, but the place where he was parked was directly between her and the hordes of shoppers, any one of whom would surely help her. She would have to wait, but she couldn't. She knew that the other man wouldn't be held up for long.

It has to be this way. Maybe he'll drive away.

She began to feel faint.

How much blood have I lost?

The van was moving, circling. Moseley kept the phone to his ear while driving. When he turned towards the shopping complex, Rachel saw her chance. She continued along the bank of the river and was just about to head in the direction of the shoppers, when the van circled again, its engine suddenly revving.

This time she was sure he had seen her. And it was only a matter of time before the other gang member caught up. Rachel went the only way she could, towards the raging river, calling for help as she limped onward. In the distance, she heard the sound of police sirens. But closer, she heard the sound of barking.

Then a gun was fired.

The bullet missed, kicked up gravel at Rachel's feet. It didn't come from Moseley, but from the man behind her. She screamed out again, but the only two people who knew where she was were Moseley and his accomplice. She had no choice... she dived into the river.

***

There was a beeping sound from the computer screen. "Moseley's sent another text, everyone," Matt exclaimed.

As soon as he spoke, it was as if he had stirred a beehive. The house began to bustle. Everywhere police and family froze, as they strained to scan the computer screen.

"Open it, son," the officer in charge instructed Matt.

Matt smoothly moved his mouse over it and double clicked, giving a nervous sigh as he did so.

After reading it, everyone was joyful.

It read, 'The girl escaped.'

Almost instantly another text appeared, 'Dog got her, she won't get far.'

This drained any hint of hope from Matt's body. Behind him, he could hear the anguished cries of his mother. He wanted to go to her, but he couldn't take his eyes off the screen in case another message would appear. It did.

'She's in the river.'

The sergeant barked into his phone, "Girl in the river. I repeat Rachel is in the river. Vicinity of Golden Island. Close in. Now!"

Another police officer had already called the emergency services and was now giving Rachel's location to the search and rescue team that was in the air.

'Girl is gone,' said the next text.

Apart from the crackle of the occasional walkie talkie, the room fell silent as everyone seemed to hold a communal breath.

Then, 'Dead, Boss. The girl is dead.'

No one could react. The finality of the words on the screen struck a blow into the hearts of those who were crowding around Matt and his computer. It was Colette who was first to respond again. The vain howl of pain she attempted to emit from lungs that were empty of air was the most pitiful that Matt had heard in his twelve short years.

"She's strong Ma, I'm sure she's still alive." He ran to his mother. "Rachel is our champion swimmer. I know she's fooling them. I just know it."

***

The instant Rachel hit the cold icy water, she knew what was coming. She had dived into the hostile waters of the river Shannon. Before she fell, she could hear police sirens in the distance, but they were too far away to help her. The last thing she had seen was Moseley, although it wasn't him who had fired the second shot at her. The zip of a bullet making its arrow line past her head told her where she was. This and the icy cold water awakened a primitive urge inside her that told her she had to survive. Now the current of the water in the murky swell of the river was wrapping its long, icy fingers around her and was pulling her down into its depths. She swallowed water before she could compose herself. Just then, images raced through her mind, as if the most important scenes of her life were flashing before her, urging her to say goodbye. In the strange, almost unconnected moment, she welcomed the invitation. Unbelievably, she saw herself standing in the dining room in Forest View, shouting at her mother. Matt's eyes were wide as he sat quietly in the corner, like a frightened mouse.

I'm sorry Mum… Then, wait, I can't leave it like this.

Then she snapped back to reality, and there was only one thing she had to do, get air.

She swam upwards, giving one last powerful kick with her aching legs, and inhaled a deep breath of air.

"Air... sweet, lovely air," Rachel rejoiced, turning worriedly to check the direction from which she had come. She was amazed at how far away it was, the only clue being the distant blue lights. She realised that she was exhausted as well as cold, and no amount of swimming would guard her from the utter, piercing chill. The violent swirls were dictating where she was going, and it wasn't in the right direction. She half swam, half treaded to get back towards the bank, fighting the fierce drag of the current. When she finally steered herself to the edge, she clawed at the reeds and exposed roots above, but her hands were no more than useless frozen claws. She cried in frustration but refused to give in. The momentum brought her towards a backwater, where a deep swirl circled before emptying its contents again out into the main body of the river. Beyond the eddy was a worn down slipway, and a green mossy bank. *This might be my last chance*, she thought, before summoning the last fibre of strength in her wracked body. She got out, painfully dragging her body up before collapsing in utter exhaustion, half in, half out of the water.

"Whoa." Rachel felt something licking her face. She rolled over.

"I'm so sorry. Cooper likes people." Standing watching her was an old man with a small dog.

"It… it's fine," she answered weakly.

"Oh dear, you don't look at all well. And look at your leg! I'd better call an ambulance!"

"No, no, please get the Guards," Rachel pleaded.

"Alright," he said and dialled their number.

Ten minutes later, Rachel thought she was in the middle of a scene from CSI. A team of medics had descended on her.

✳✳✳

When the call came over the police radio, everyone jumped. Superintendent Finlay beamed as he turned and gave the thumbs up to the grief-filled group in the sitting room. He appealed for calm only to lose it again when he announced, "She's safe!"

As soon as he had regained a semblance of decorum, Finlay continued to relay the message he had just received.

"They're mystified as to how anyone could make it through the current, but Rachel did it. She got out. She was washed up a half mile below Athlone, and apart from a few cuts and bruises and a nasty dog bite, she's not badly hurt. She is suffering from hypothermia, though, and they are taking her to Tullamore Hospital."

The ringing of Colette's phone surprised no one. Again the surveillance team leapt into action.

"Play along, Ronan. Let them make their play. And remember, spin it out this time," Finlay emphasised.

Following the same directions as earlier, Ronan waited until the phone had nearly rung out before answering.

"You took your sweet little time there, Ronan. That little stunt won't work and your friends can search all they want. We've moved Rachel to a much safer place."

"So, what's the plan?" Ronan asked, much to the frustration of Finlay.

Ronan shot him the kind of look that suggested that he was in charge of the conversation, before turning his back and addressing his enemy.

"My daughter had better be safe..."

"You know the gravel quarries between you and Tullamore?"

"Which one?"

"Elves Quarry."

"Yes, I know it."

"That's where we'll do it. You bring the case with the jewels in it. If you come on your own, I will give you back your daughter. But remember, if we hear so much as an ambulance siren, your feisty little girl will be no more. Do you understand me?"

"I understand."

"That's more like it now, Ronan. You have exactly thirty minutes."

"Drat," Finlay said. "That doesn't give us much time. Why did they pick a quarry of all places?"

"Easy to get out of, overland, even by water. Quarries, woods, back roads and about ten different directions they can take when they get what it is they want," Ronan supplied. "It's not as stupid as it sounds." He sounded confident. Turning to Agatha, he said, "Let's give them what they want, Aggie. You still have my suitcases, I presume?"

"Both of them, Master Ronan, the real one and the fake one. Safe and sound in the strong room," she smiled, pushing her heavy glasses up onto the bridge of her nose. She reached for her tea caddy and to an audience of curious glances, emptied its contents carefully out onto a linen cloth before uncovering a key. Her onlookers became even more engrossed as she moved a picture on the wall to reveal a well-recessed wall safe. Out of this, she fished an even bigger key.

"I'm not to be followed now, when I go into the parlour," she ordered. "Not even policemen are allowed in here and I mean it."

"Especially not policemen," Superintendent Finlay quipped, making everyone laugh as Agatha took the key of her parlour out of the large pocket in the front of her house coat.

"Oh ye're all very smart now aren't ye?" Agatha retorted, not appreciating the joke. She disappeared from view.

Her key turned in the lock from the other side of the door, enforcing her insistence on privacy. After what seemed an eternity, Agatha emerged with a black brief case which she handed to Ronan. As he tried to take it from her, she held its handle long enough to pull him down to her and kiss him on the cheek. "May God be with you and keep you from all harm, Ronan."

"Thanks aunty Aggie," he said before turning to the commanding officer. "Right, let's do this."

"We already have the rapid response units covering all the main roads and we have the Garda sub aqua vessels with armed men on board making their way down the Shannon and up the River Brosna just in case they have a boat. We have the best snipers in the country moving in overland in case they try and take you out, which they will try to do when this thing goes south, make no mistake. Here put this on," Finlay said, handing Ronan a protective vest.

Before he left, Ronan turned to his family. Matt led the way by giving him a lingering hug before Colette approached cautiously, with a shorter embrace.

Matt said, "Be careful, Dad."

"That goes for me too," Colette managed, before her husband was whisked away by a scrum of police men and women.

Five minutes later, Agatha broke the tension of the waiting group, shouting from her parlour, "Dear Lord have mercy on me".

She emerged in the doorway with a partially open briefcase in her hands. "I was sure the O'Connor Crown was in the one with the black handle, but it is the other way around. And aren't I after handing the wrong one to poor Ronan. God forgive me, but I am after sending him off with the very thing I was sworn to protect. What sort of a stupid old woman am I?"

"Don't worry, Agatha," Matt reassured her, "those robbers won't get anywhere near our precious jewels. My dad will make sure of that." He turned to the policemen who were left to guard the group, "Can you radio them and let them know?" he asked the nearest one to him.

"Sure son, but it will have to be by phone. We don't have a walkie talkie now. They've taken both of them with them." He began to dial. Then, "The chief is not picking up, I'll try one of the others. Problem is that they may have put phones on silent on a job like this. It's standard procedure. Don't worry though, I'll call the station." He walked outside.

***

Elves Quarry consisted of a two-mile-long network of excavated sand pits and quarries, which had long since given up their limestone and gravel deposits. The system ran into a low-lying flood plain that became treacherous each year when the river Brosna burst its banks and turned the entire place into one vast, dangerous lake. The disturbance of the ancient maze of underground limestone caves, which had been destroyed in the years of industrial pillage, caused the loss of many lives down the years. As a result, Elves Quarry had long been a no-go area for the youngsters of the surrounding villages. Parents preached to their children to keep away. If the signs warning people to keep out didn't work, the stories of hauntings and alleged sightings of previous lost souls certainly did the trick for all but the very adventurous, or foolhardy.

It was to this place that Ronan O'Connor now drove his wife's limping car, in the hope of finally putting a sad chapter of his past behind him. Safe in the knowledge that he was trading nothing for nothing, he smiled as he neared the barren lake system that supported very little by way of life and served no purpose now other than simply being there. If it helped him rid himself and his family of this gang, which had never stopped planning to destroy him and end his reign as protector of the legacy he was born to defend, he would celebrate the place forever. The piece in his ear buzzed. It was a minder, requesting that Ronan slow down a little to allow the right people to get in place. The third call, from the man they had come to know as Moseley, told him which approach road to take. Ronan found it infuriating that the man's picture came up on the phone every time he called Colette's number. How the worm had infiltrated his family to its core! A deep anger stirred within him. He was certain that he would surely kill Ricky Molloy if the chance presented itself.

Now, as he took the road locally known as Tara Lane, he knew that the police couldn't possibly cover all the exits. The old revolver he had asked Agatha to place under the seat was a comfort to him, all the more so when he was diverted off the road by a fallen tree and a young thug appeared, directing him by waving his sawn-off shotgun.

Not doing hitch hikers right now, Sonny. Ronan slowed now, watching in his rear view mirror. The youth ran a few yards after his car and threatened to shoot, before apparently thinking better of it and slinking into the trees and down the slope towards the water. *Bet he hasn't acquainted himself with the local folklore and the dangers of these parts.* Ronan checked the revolver that hadn't been fired in seven years. *Don't let me down now if I need you, Betsy,* he said to the ancient piece. With the weapon checked, he spoke into the tiny microphone that was inserted into his shirt collar.

"Just turned left off Tara Lane. Moving slowly in the direction of the abandoned quarry office. Already got directions from a friendly soul with a shotgun, not sure if he wanted a lift." There was no reply. "Anyone there?" Again, there was nothing.

As it was only five hundred yards to the old office building, Ronan drove more than half way there, long enough to shake his young pursuer, before abandoning the car, taking the gun and the briefcase, and diving up the slope to his left. Moving forward under the cover of a roadside bank of earth, he soon sighted the building that was surely earmarked for the meeting place. A blue van was parked in plain sight, its rear doors ajar. Beyond the works office, Ronan saw a large speedboat with a driver at the rudder, poised and ready. *So that's your plan, is it?*

"They have a boat," he whispered into his microphone; but again, nothing came back. Then a crackling sound nearly deafened him.

It was loud enough to be heard by others. The sound of a breaking twig below and behind him confirmed that someone was on to him. Leaving the crackling device hanging on a branch, Ronan crawled up the slope and behind a large mass of boulders just feet away, to await his prey.

It took less than a minute for the shotgun-carrying youth to turn up, only to find himself on the receiving end of a large boulder to the head, from which even his thick hoodie couldn't protect him. Throwing down the case, Ronan raised his stunned victim to his feet and marched him back onto the road. *Time to attract a little attention,* he thought, firing a single shot into the air. The crack of the revolver, as well as driving birds from the trees all around, had the unfortunate consequence of alerting another sentry who was following in the footsteps of his hooded friend. This one emerged from behind Ronan just as he heard the powerful engine of the motorboat fire into life.

The shotgun blast caught Ronan in the shoulder and his captive in the back of the head, just below the ear. It sent them both spinning to the dirt before Ronan could compose himself long enough to squeeze off a round at the man behind him. He missed.

When the shooter approached, carrying the briefcase in one hand and a double-barrelled sawn off shotgun in the other, Ronan recognised the man on the phone. The youth at his side began to moan and drag himself up. Time seemed to freeze as Moseley and Ronan eyed each other, seven years of shared hatred was pent up in their pointed weapons.

"Here," Moseley shouted to the youth, "take the case and get into the boat." He turned to Ronan. "Aren't you going to ask me where the girl is? No? Well, she's half way to Limerick by now, only somewhere at the bottom of the river," he sneered, raising the gun to point it directly at Ronan's head.

"She's..." Ronan began, only to be cut off by the sharp crack of a sniper's rifle. The headshot ended Moseley's speech, freezing his leering grin into a death mask, causing him to sag and fall as if all life had instantly been sucked from him.

Propping himself up on his good elbow, Ronan turned to see the boat power out across the blue lake before a bullet pierced its inflatable side. It limped on, but the marksman was good, each discharge from his high-powered rifle sinking the craft further and further into the water until the engine gave up, unable to push the ball of rubber that had formerly been a boat around in circles, before crew and vessel sunk from view. His last sight was of a Garda craft rescuing the two struggling gang members before the pain hit him.

My family is safe and the crown jewels are safe. Now I will have to pay my dues, he thought as he lost consciousness.

- 23 -

THE CUSTODIAN

T he security guard nodded respectfully as Colette and Matt walked past him into the isolation room that had been specially set up for Rachel and Ronan O'Connor. After two days of treatment, they were both ready for discharge. Ronan had almost needed the resuscitation machine on the previous day when he was well enough to be told that his precious family heirloom was lying somewhere at the bottom of Elves Quarry. A subsequent report that it had been fished out and sent to the National Museum for restoration and safekeeping did little to alleviate his stress levels.

It was Colette who had eventually made him lighten up with a sharp lecture on his priorities. Ronan had no choice but to agree after both his children joined in.

Now Colette breezed in. Her smile radiated a new-found confidence, and her hair shone as she swished it with aplomb.

"How are we all doing this morning?" she asked, kissing both patients in turn.

"Terrible," Rachel moaned playfully. "I can't stick one more night of that old man's snoring. I'm going to sue this hospital for putting me in here."

"If she doesn't sue, I will. I've had to put up with vibrating phones, constant Facebook updates from all her ten thousand fans and well-wishers. And if the social media isn't humming, then the so-called music coming out of those headphones is polluting the atmosphere in here."

"At least I'm only polluting the atmosphere, he's polluting..."

"So you have been getting along famously then?" Colette chirped, ignoring the half-hearted complaints.

"Mum and I have had to slum it in the Bridge House Hotel until the guards decide it's safe to go back to the house," Matt said. "Oh and Mr Freckles too, of course. He wants me to book the main ballroom for a show. The manager, Noel McCann, is a real nice man. He says that if we're good enough he'll give us a slot. We can do loads of mind reading stuff and..."

"Now Matt," said Colette, "steady on there. I'm not so sure if this dummy business is good for you. And if you two think you have it bad putting up with each other, you should try sharing a suite with a twelve-year-old boy and his constantly think-talking two-hundred-year-old friend. Now if that's not enough to drive a body back onto the Valium then..."

"Oh no, you won't!" Matt and Rachel chorused together.

"Look on the bright side, Mum," Rachel said, "at least Matt is now Mister Confidence instead of the brow beaten wimp we had before."

"Does that mean that I'll be looking after my big sister at school, seeing as you will be on those crutches for a while?"

"If you're lucky, I'll let you carry my bag... but only as far as the front gates. I should have lots of offers from there on," Rachel laughed.

"I should have known, some things would never change." Matt said, accepting that his sister was still the boss.

***

It was a happy afternoon when Rachel and Ronan were released from Tullamore General Hospital, having been treated for what turned out to be no more than superficial wounds. Matt, Rachel, Freckles, David, Colette and Ronan walked from where they had parked at Durrow Abbey towards Agatha's house, where they were invited for supper. Agatha informed them that her new butler, Gabriel, would be helping her serve high tea.

The warm, sparkling sun seemed to reflect their mood.

As they walked to the lodge, Colette chatted to Agatha on the phone, telling her not to go to too much trouble. David was deeply engrossed in his surroundings. According to him, everything was cool.

Matt was walking along, hand in hand with his father. Rachel was on Ronan's good side, leaning heavily on him. They were laughing and talking, just happy to be together, as they had been over seven years ago.

As they mounted the steps to the raised veranda, Matt's backpack started moving as Mr Freckles began to struggle inside.

Let me out of here, it is most confining. If I were human I am sure I would be claustrophobic.

Matt fished him out of his bag.

"Ah Ronan. I don't believe we have been formally reacquainted," Matt said on Mr Freckles' behalf, his lips barely moving.

"It's good to see you too, Tickles."

"It is Freckles now. Freckles Shackleton is my full name, much more sophisticated, don't you think?" Matt supplied.

"I see, how distinguished. What ever happened to Tickles O'Connor? Are we not good enough for you now?" said Ronan, a little uncomfortable as Colette looked back with a "don't-tell-me-you're-at-it-too," gaze.

"Anyway," said Matt, knowing when to stop, "are we going to move back to Durrow Abbey?"

With a smile Ronan said, "I thought you'd never ask".

I think that decision would be most wise. It is the ancestral seat after all. Matt repeated what his wooden friend had said. Everyone laughed.

"Would that decision have anything to do with a certain woman in the gatekeeper's lodge?" asked Ronan knowingly.

If carved wooden faces could blush, Freckles' would have been as red as a tomato.

"Ew, gross," said Matt.

Ronan paused on the doorstep of Agatha's house. He looked up at the detailed crown embossed on the stone plaque on the wall. Then he stared straight into Matt's eyes and grabbed his shoulders. "Do you know what this means?" he asked.

Agatha has the fire lit? Freckles offered, looking at the smoke rising from the chimney. Then, *I love a nice fire. Agatha is so considerate. Oh wait! I am a fire hazard, how could she?*

"What does it mean, Dad?"

Ronan smiled and looked at Matt, "You are now the custodian."